BEACH BREEZES

Cas Dunlap

Also by Cas Dunlap

Southern Lights
It's News To Us

The characters and events in this book are fictitious. Any similarity to real persons, living or dead, is coincidental and is not intended by the author.

New South Press • Pensacola, Florida
First Edition 1999

ISBN 0-967-04202-X

10 9 8 7 6 5 4 3 2 1

Dedication

To my wife Anne, who suffers gently a writer's ego while editing my work into a much better book.

ACKNOWLEDGEMENTS

Thanks to Hugh Armstrong for his brilliant cover art; to Kathy Tanner for the tour of local environs; to the Escambia County Sheriff's Department – especially Lisa Lagergren, Capt. Dottie Way, and Lt. Buck Poythress – for a touch of authenticity; and to John Keliher for his unique insight.

Foreword

If you didn't read my first beach book, *Southern Lights*, don't worry about it. *Beach Breezes* isn't, strictly speaking, a sequel. I've brought some of the characters back for the sake of continuity, but basically these are new people – I hope you'll like them as well – in a new adventure. Like *Southern Lights*, *Beach Breezes* will not give you a headache. It's another beach book meant to entertain and set in God's gift to the planet – Pensacola Beach.

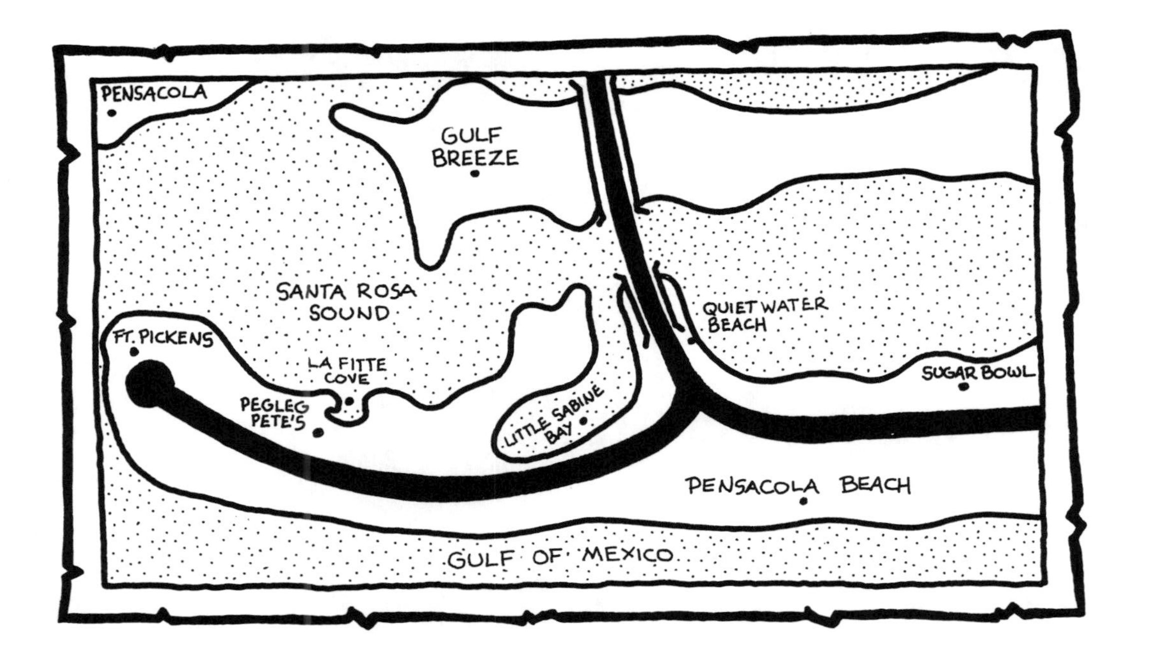
PENSACOLA
GULF BREEZE
SANTA ROSA SOUND
FT. PICKENS
LA FITTE COVE
PEGLEG PETE'S
LITTLE SABINE BAY
QUIET WATER BEACH
SUGAR BOWL
PENSACOLA BEACH
GULF OF MEXICO

BEACH BREEZES

CHAPTER 1

Charlie Cross lay sprawled in the cockpit of his thirty-five-foot sloop.

Earlier he had planned to do something, but as he made his preparations to go out for the night, a brilliant full moon was rising over the Gulf of Mexico, coincident with a gentle wind soothingly rocking his boat. Charlie decided it was one of those rare August nights when it was not too cool and not too hot, but just right, mentally quoting Goldilocks. Instead of heading up the dock to Peg Leg Pete's Oyster Bar to find whatever fun might be available, he had opted to kick back, lower the bimini, and let the natural beauty of the Gulf Coast night flow around him.

Apparently he'd been tired, for now he awoke, feeling slightly dew-soaked, to the voices from the next slip. The moon had vanished in the overcast, and the chill of the night signaled that it was time to go below. Whoever was in the boat next to his hadn't noticed the sleeping man, as they now carried on a conversation that Charlie figured wasn't meant for his ears.

"Sure it'd get more attention if we waited 'til it was half up, and then blew hell outta it, but I say we can't wait. We gotta fight the bastards ever' step of the way," hissed a raspy male voice.

"Yeah, well, that may be fine, but if we start just damagin' things, they'ah goin' ta think it's kid stuff. They'll double up security, and then we'll have trouble doin' anythin'," another, slightly accented, voice intoned.

"Tim's right." A third point of view was voiced. "If we let 'em go right along, other developers are gonna see what an easy time they're havin', and start up the same routine with the commissioners, pushin' for some cockamamie variance for another high-rise. We gotta let 'em know it's not gonna be a piece of cake if they start to build."

A bass tone silenced the others. "All your opinions have merit in my judgment. Perhaps some form of compromise is in order." There was silence, as the others seemed to wait for directions. "Suppose, for instance, occasional major damage was done, enough to get their attention and anyone else's who might be watching, but not enough to completely halt their progress. Then, when the superstructure's in place, the *coup de grace*. The lesson being: the going will be hard and then it gets worse; no profit to be made here."

Silence again ensued – the conspirators must have been mulling over the new plan. Then, "Yeah, the Colonel's right. I think that's the way to go." This was followed by a round of assent from all the voices previously heard.

Charlie, whose initial reaction was to sit up and make some kind of noise to alert the little group to his presence before things went too far, realized things had now gone beyond that point, and that it was imperative they not notice him. He thought about crawling down the companionway; but, in the dark, he might easily make some noise that would expose his presence. He had never been a tidy person – who knew where he might have left an empty beer can or an unused bucket to stumble over? No, the best plan was to just lie still. Maybe they wouldn't notice him at all, and, if they did, he could feign sleep.

The bass voice was continuing. "OK, it's agreed. For now, that's enough. We'll meet again later this week to work out the details of our first strike. In the meantime, be thinking about what mischief we might do. I'll contact you in the usual way. And keep this in mind: we're not playing games here. If any of this comes to light, the only water we'll see for many years is whatever the State of Florida provides in our cells. Do I make myself clear on that point?"

Each voice answered in the affirmative, as if the man with the bass voice was locking eyes with one after another. Then the scuttling of feet. They were going somewhere. Charlie's moment of peril was now.

On a still night, men clamoring from a boat can make an incredible amount of noise. But that was good, Charlie reasoned. As long as they were bumping and thumping, they weren't paying any attention to him.

Then, "Hey, look at that!"

Oh, shit, thought Charlie, pretending for all he was worth to be sound asleep.

The heretofore indiscriminate noise had quieted. Then Charlie heard the noise of feet gently shuffling. He could almost feel their eyes as they each evaluated what threat, if any, Charlie presented.

Then, "Looks like he's sleeping" came the whisper, and nothing.

"Hmmm," sounded the bass voice.

This would be it, Charlie figured. Bass Voice was calling the shots, and whatever he decided, the others would accept. After more quiet time, the sound of footsteps moving away floated in the night air.

Charlie's first feeling was relief – Whew! I think I'll have a beer and hit the rack. On second thought, though, he reasoned that if he were in Bass Voice's place, he would pretend to leave and station a man behind to watch for any evidence that Charlie had been faking. If he hadn't been hallucinating, the stakes in this game were too high to leave the question of being overheard to chance. Charlie wished now he had brought a blanket up from the cabin earlier. It would be a long chilly night, but there was no way he was going to trade his life for a better place to sleep.

As the minutes slowly ticked to hours, Charlie was left alone with his thoughts – waiting for the axe to fall was not conducive to sleep.

Initially, he just lay still and listened. What would be the telltale noises that might betray the assailant, if he decided Charlie had to go? Assuming, of course, there was an assailant. For all he knew, the little group had just walked off, and all of them were now snug in bed.

But no, he was right to be cautious. These boys weren't foolin' around, and they knew the risks. Given that, Charlie could only figure they wouldn't jeopardize their mission and themselves, even if it meant murder.

As he lay listening, he reviewed all the potential defense weapons at his disposal. Obviously, the best one was the .38 Smith & Wesson under his mattress in the cabin. If he heard an intruder soon enough, he thought he might have a good chance of getting to it. Once down the companionway and into the dark cabin, he had the advantage. He knew the boat; the intruder didn't. But, of course, that only worked if he had time. If he never heard the guy, or if the guy elected to stand on the dock and shoot him ... Well, if that was how it was going to play out, he might as well go to sleep.

Best scenario was that he had enough time. Then he'd win. Next best scenario was that he had some time, and what? Charlie strained his brain: what had he done with the jib winch handle? If it was in the hatch, he could use it as a weapon. If he'd decided to neaten up, it would be downstairs somewhere near the gun. No help. He resolved never to neaten up again.

It was no use; he couldn't remember. If that's how it came down, he'd try for the winch handle, and if it wasn't there, he'd go *mano a mano*. Odds were, though, the guy would have some kind of cutting weapon. Hell, if he was going to shoot Charlie, why not just do it from the dock?

The question then was, what could Charlie do against a man with a knife? And the answer was, probably get killed. Flirting with the half-century mark, Charlie wasn't the man he used to be, and even that younger man wouldn't have fared well against a knife.

Charlie decided the best course of action, if he had limited time, was to jump in the water, and hope he could swim faster than whoever wanted him dead.

Having resolved his contingency plans, he wondered whether changing positions was a sign of sleep or not. What the hell, it seemed like the thing to do, and besides that, he was getting a cramp in his leg. He debated moaning when he moved, but discarded that as too theatrical. Then he waited ... Nothing. Good.

Drifting to the conversation he had heard, Charlie concluded that these people were going to do serious harm to the newly approved Sandcastle Beach Hotel and Condominiums, the newest twenty-five-story high-rise condo complex to be approved for Pensacola Beach by the county commissioners. Charlie knew no right-thinking American wanted to see this monstrosity come to dwarf the little beach community, but blowing it up was a bit extreme. Why would a person do that?

As he pondered that question, Charlie must have finally dozed, for he awoke with a start to the leering eyes of the ugliest gray crane he had ever seen. After checking to make sure that his heart hadn't, in fact, stopped, he was relieved to see the first remnants of dawn creeping around the Santa Rosa Towers. He never thought he'd be relieved to see a high-rise, but this was an exception. If the assailant was still there, he'd just have to take it on faith that Charlie was an early riser.

As sunlight banished the dark corners and cobwebs, Charlie wondered if anything really significant had happened, or if he had just overreacted to some silly men playing some kind of weird game.

CHAPTER 2

Charles Travis Cross hadn't always been "Charlie." The nickname just seemed right when he got it, and now especially after he'd lived at the beach for a few years. "Charlie" was a good guy, a guy to drink beer with, go fishing with, a fun kind of person. "Charles" wasn't. "Charles" was a stuffy civil lawyer, a financial manager, a bank president, a person to be reckoned with.

Charlie's dad had wanted Charlie to be known as Travis, because Charlie's dad bled University of Texas burnt orange, and considered it one of the highest of all possible honors to be named after one of the heroes of the Alamo. However, the best laid plans can be demolished by a first grade teacher. A nun named Sister Mary David decided that the young bespectacled Travis was a Charles, and that was that. The teacher called him Charles, therefore his classmates called him Charles. Finally, even his dad acquiesced.

Regardless of whether the chicken was

necessary to produce the egg, or the egg was first necessary to produce the chicken, young Master Cross was on the "Charles" track, and there he stayed for most of his life.

Charles was both intellectually and physically gifted. But he also possessed, perhaps was possessed by, another component of personality that causes cream to rise – he was driven. It wasn't that Mr. or Mrs. Cross pushed the boy. In fact, Mr. Cross should have been named Charlie, as in "good time." Financially secure, Mr. Cross spent much of his time sailing, a skill he passed on to Charles. Maybe that was it; Charles reacted to his dad. Maybe it was the nuns. For whatever reason, it became critical for Charles to be Number One, and he put in the time to make it so.

When other kids watched TV, Charles studied. When other kids played games, Charles worked on technique: pitch, pass, dribble. Charles's idea of diversion was martial arts in the off-season, when once upon a time sports had an off-season. And in the end, or maybe somewhere in the middle, it paid off – kind of. Graduating first in his high school class led to acceptance at an Ivy League college, which led to acceptance at a prestigious law school, which led to a job at a top law firm on the partner track. What with double promotions and heavy academic loads, this was all accomplished by the ripe old age of twenty-two. Along the way Charles was Mister All Everything in sports, which helped out in the area where Charles had no experience: the opposite sex.

Charles had the good fortune to meet Amelia Sue Putnam at a mixer, sponsored by his law school and a nearby women's college, during his last year of law school. At least, that's the way Charles saw it. The truth of the matter was that Charles, being everybody's choice for most likely to be a really good provider, was snagged, bagged, and tagged at the mixer. Thereafter, he was properly trained.

At age twenty-four, Charles had a promising career as a probate attorney, putting in eighty or so hours a week. Amelia Sue busied herself spending the money Charles brought home and trying to have children. For better or for worse, either Charles or Amelia was not fertile. This problem didn't bother Charles much; he was enjoying the effort. Amelia, on the other hand, was beside herself. To her way of thinking, no children meant not much of a marriage at all. Nevertheless, she persevered.

It was at this point that Charles's run of luck began to turn, whether for good or bad was debatable. For years, the war in Southeast Asia had been raging. Neither Charles nor Amelia had paid much attention; it didn't really concern them. Charles was in college, then law school, and so was accorded a deferment. Now, though, he was no longer in school, and being married with no children made him eligible to do his duty.

Being a pretty smart fellow, this circumstance had not escaped Charles. One of the senior partners in the firm had a friend on the draft board, so when it looked like a sure thing that Charles's number would be called, word of same was communicated to Charles. Since flying an airplane looked a lot better to Charles than crawling around in the jungle, he joined the Navy in hopes of becoming a naval aviator.

Although Charles would have liked to get this chore out of the way as quickly as possible, the Navy had other ideas. The Navy had no wish to train Charles to fly jets, only to have him bail out after four years; if Charles wanted to fly, an eight-year hitch was mandatory.

To Charles, this was just another challenge. To Amelia, eight years out of their lives was lunacy. Amelia's moaning, bitching, and cajoling notwithstanding, lunacy prevailed.

In the Navy, Charles gradually became

Charlie, and Charlie loved the camaraderie and the flying. What Charlie didn't love were the things he saw and experienced during the war, even though it ended shortly after his arrival in Viet Nam. Death and suffering had heretofore been something in the newspaper. Having seen as many John Wayne movies as the next American, Charlie found the reality of war shocking, to put it mildly. Eight years later, not only had Charles become Charlie, but something in him had changed. Like the warm days of September, the calendar still says it's summer, but something almost indefinable is different.

Amelia was waiting. The law firm was waiting. All that remained for Charlie to do was get up to speed and take up where he'd left off, and this Charlie did like the trooper he was. In fact, after a year and a half, he made partner; looking in from the outside, things were perfect.

On the inside, things were a bit different. Amelia still wanted children, but since the Navy hadn't changed their basic chemistry, none were forthcoming. As a result, Amelia had insisted they go to a fertility clinic, and Charlie had complied – reluctantly. Charlie was not sure he wanted to bring children into this world. In addition, it became increasingly clear that, whereas Amelia was a champagne-caviar-and-charity-ball type of lady, Charlie was a beer-pizza-and-rented-video kind of guy.

At the firm, things were going well, but not exactly like Charlie had supposed they would. He had always figured that a person busted his ass on one stair to make it to the next, but that at some point there was a plateau where a person could relax a bit and reap the rewards of his effort. It seemed that the firm's idea of how things worked was that a new associate put in eighty hours a week to make partner so he could continue putting in eighty hours a week. The only thing that changed was the money.

One Tuesday morning, as the sun broke over a billboard that featured tan bikini-clad women dangling from a sloop in full sail on the emerald waters of the Caribbean, Charlie sat stuck in freeway traffic. It wasn't necessary to look to his left and right. He knew that if he did, he would see his mirror image: beady-eyed bewhiskered rodents racing for the city. The day would go as most days went, ending around seven in the evening with Charlie mentally whipped. This evening he would have just enough time to get home, change into his tuxedo, and race with Amelia back downtown to the celebrity banquet that launched a fund drive for something that he couldn't remember.

Charlie had always had a theory about why people do things. The gist of the idea was that people do things they like to do, and don't do things they don't like to do. All things – other people, jobs, games, places – have a positive or negative value, and if the positive value exceeds the negative value, a person likes that person, does that job, plays that game, goes to that place. On the other hand, if the thing acquires a negative value, a person doesn't live with that person anymore, do that thing anymore, and on and on. A person's environment and all the things in it are just a collection of little pluses and little minuses, and as the balance shifts from positive to negative or negative to positive, the person moves toward or away from whatever it is. At the next exit, he got off.

After halfheartedly suggesting that Charlie see a shrink, Amelia agreed that a fifty-fifty split of all their assets seemed fair, if Charlie would also take the liabilities. The senior partner to whom Charlie reported merely nodded and wished him luck. This was not a novel turn of events for the firm.

After the divorce was final, Charlie had just enough money to buy a sailboat, the *Long Gone*, and head for the last place he had been happy – N.A.S. Pensacola, where he had trained to be a naval aviator.

As luck would have it, the Gulf of Mexico was relatively calm. So the run from Houston to Pensacola Beach wasn't much of a trick. He hadn't bothered to call LaFitte Cove Marina to check on the availability of a slip – in his new life, Charlie would act on impulse and let fate sort things out. Besides, it was autumn and that meant the summer slip renters would have gone elsewhere.

As he slid through Pensacola Pass, Charlie managed to raise the harbor master on the radio – no mean feat – and sure enough, there was a slip available right in back of Peg Leg Pete's.

Time had passed in a haze since Charlie's arrival date, and he had easily made the transition from high-powered lawyer to beach person, called a Wooliebooger by some locals.

For money, he did odd jobs, mostly repaired boats for those owners who only knew how to drive them. Because cold beer and assorted fried fish things were way too convenient, he had added a new dimension to his frontal silhouette. He had a pretty good relationship with a local shell artist who lived in a rented house facing the gulf. Life was good.

At least, that was true until the night of the four strangers.

CHAPTER 3

Even in early September, it didn't take much sunshine to warm Santa Rosa Island, home of Pensacola Beach, from a chill through the "real comfortable" zone and into the "move to the shade or start sweating" area of the thermostat.

Charlie had had over three weeks now to dismiss from his mind the peculiar event of the four strangers, and, at this point in his day, his major concern was some chocolate milk and a newspaper. A couple of aspirins would have been nice as well, but he had forgotten to buy any during his weekly pilgrimage to America, as the beach locals referred to the real City of Pensacola. Now the intensity of his headache did not merit wasting money he had tagged for necessities: beer and food.

As Charlie sat in the "UnderWhere" section of Peg Leg's – the owner didn't care if Charlie sat there until it was time to open for business – he felt irrationally proud of himself. One more time, he had successfully negotiated the perilous journey from his slip through Peg Leg's parking lot to the Tom Thumb and back. It was perilous because Charlie's flip-flops were about gone and Peg Leg's parking lot was like a battlefield littered with aging oyster shells.

Flipping to the editorial page of the *Pensacola News Journal,* Charlie noted with approval that the controversy still raged about funeral etiquette in traffic. By his count of letters to the editor, the pull-over-and-stop-as-a-gesture-of-respect people were trashing the I'm-in-too-damn-big-of-a-hurry-to-care group. This was a good thing. He couldn't imagine people in a big city, even a southern big city, caring enough about that kind of issue to write letters to their newspaper, or the newspaper itself caring enough to publish them for that matter. He loved Pensacola.

After a long slow sip of chocolate milk, his attention was drawn to the major boldface:

SECURITY GUARD FOUND DEAD AT BUILDING SITE

Construction workers reporting to the jobsite of the soon-to-be tallest high-rise structure on Pensacola Beach were greeted with evidence of a grisly crime. The

> decapitated body of local security guard, Hulen Puckett, age 78, was found near the burned carcass of an earthmoving machine.
>
> Sheriff Slidell Goodbee indicated that it was too soon to say whether the death was a homicide, but that his department would continue to investigate.
>
> Puckett was a life-long resident of Milton, who had served honorably in World War ...

The article went on to detail the life and times of Hulen Puckett, but had little else to say about the alleged crime. This was fine with Charlie, whose eyes had glazed over as chocolate milk ran down his chin. As it stood now, thought Charlie, the whole thing could be some weird coincidence.

Had he known the truth, he would probably have gone straight upstairs for a cold beer or something stronger.

*****

The Wooliebooger Militia, as they styled themselves, had convened at the stroke of midnight the night before at the house of their leader, Colonel Ruston Dubach, United States Army (Retired). The entire militia consisted of four guys, who were relatively longtime residents of the island, and who were bound together by their mutual love for Wednesday night poker and their mutual hate for anything that might destroy the laid-back simplicity of Pensacola Beach.

It was Chou Sibley, the accountant and youngest member of the militia, who had suggested their leading gambit. "Ah thank we should put mothballs in thea gas tanks," he drawled, in a soft Alabama accent.

This had seemed reasonable enough to the others, albeit somewhat adolescent, and the execution of the plan had been simple enough.

Having gathered at the Colonel's modest cinderblock home on the sound side of the island, they had donned commando garb, blacked their faces, and set out in an old whaler the Colonel kept tied up at his dock. Beaching the craft farther east, where the initial excavation for the condo project was taking place, they silently crept to the bulldozer nearest the shore, opened the gas tank, and poured in a handful of mothballs. As they nodded with satisfaction at one another, their scheme suddenly turned south.

From out of nowhere came Hulen Puckett, shining a flashlight precisely in their direction. It was now fight or run, and the mighty militia chose the latter, scampering off in the direction of the whaler.

Approaching as rapidly as an elderly man could approach, Hulen tripped on a newly dug rut, spilling himself and his flashlight hard on the sand. Getting up, Hulen discovered that he was none the worse for wear, but his flashlight had been irreparably damaged. Hulen continued more cautiously, duty-bound to investigate whatever skullduggery might be taking place on his watch.

Hulen, a man attuned to the news, had noted with disapproval the apparent epidemic of graffiti which was fast becoming a blight on the world. That incident in Singapore involving the caning of an American boy seemed to Hulen to be not nearly enough punishment for that type of senseless vandalism. Now he was sure, as he approached the dozer, that this was just the type thing he was thwarting.

Unfortunately, Hulen's eyesight was failing, and now he had lost his flashlight. Being ever resourceful, he struck a match in the unusually calm night air to investigate the damage done. He was about to conclude that he had arrived in the nick of time to ward off the vandals, when his match hand passed over the dozer's gas tank. Because his eyesight made it necessary to get close to the match while holding the match very close to the area investigated, when the tank exploded, Hulen's head, absent his body, was sent in the direction of Gulf Breeze.

*****

The Wooliebooger Militia wasn't exactly the Wild Bunch; more like the Appledumpling Gang. All of them lived happily at the beach, *sans* spouse. Three were retired military, and one, Choudrant Sibley, had a real job in Pensacola.

Choudrant Sibley, who was real quick to tell anyone his nickname was pronounced "shoe" and not "chow", was the product of a father from the now almost-gone little town of Repton in southern Alabama and his French war bride, Genevieve Devereaux. Educated at the University of Southern Mississippi, Chou drifted south to Pensacola for want of anyplace else to go and because he got a job in the accounting section of a large paper mill. Oddly mature for his age, he found social life in the city boring. In fact, the only thing Chou liked about the area was the barrier island of Santa Rosa.

Chou worked hard for the paper mill, and gradually accumulated a good deal of responsibility. The wage was sufficient to allow the purchase of a condominium on the island – facing the Gulf of Mexico, in the central area of Pensacola Beach – and this was Chou's special place in life. All the troubles and frustrations lifted from his consciousness almost magically as he passed over the Bob Sikes Bridge from the mainland to the island everyday.

The things that interested Chou in life – the sea, its wildlife, and his job – were quite sufficient without another person to share them. As far as he was concerned, his solitary lifestyle could have gone on forever. And it might have, absent Island Quest, Inc., sarcastically nicknamed IQ by the beach citizenry because they thought it was a stupid outfit.

IQ was a shell corporation created specifically to do all things necessary to develop a twenty-five-story high-rise condominium and accompanying resort compound community at the east end of Pensacola Beach. This got Chou's attention. It was the impetus for his involvement in the politics of the Santa Rosa Island Authority, the SRIA for short, and how he chanced on Colonel Ruston Dubach at an SRIA open meeting.

From Colonel Dubach's opposition to the pending development, it was clear to Chou that the

Colonel was a kindred spirit with whom he should align himself. Colonel Dubach did not disabuse Chou of that notion.

Colonel Ruston Dubach, the *kahuna* of the Wooliebooger Militia, was a product of Virginia Military Institute, World War II, Korea, and Viet Nam. Somewhere in the process of all this, he became a leader of men, but unfortunately lost his children and a wife named Hildy to what the Colonel characterized as a "limpwristed pinko academic puke."

In his career, Colonel Dubach had seen all he wanted to see of ego-driven acquisition at the expense of the innocent. Being a student of history, he didn't really see the end of such shenanigans. But he had hoped that, after retirement, he could find someplace where power struggles had not reached – a place mellow and unpretentious – a place like Pensacola Beach. Despite these feelings, he retained and encouraged the use of the title Colonel.

Even given internal contradictions, Colonel Dubach was a happy man. He liked the ocean. He liked hanging out at Bobby D's Beach Bar. He liked playing poker on Wednesday nights. He liked the Blue Angels. He primarily, though, liked it when things were going the way he wanted them to go, and at this point, life was to his liking.

At least it was until two things occurred that upset his balance. These things were, as he frequently said, "the goddamned idiot Navy transferred our poker fourth to Guam, and some megalomaniac developer started a skyscraper in my backyard." The introduction of Choudrant Sibley on the scene seemed efficacious to the amelioration of both problems.

The last two members of the militia were Thomas and Timothy Riley. The Rileys were twins, born in Boston – Chelsea Naval Hospital to be exact – and raised in various Navy towns, eventually transplanted to Pensacola when their father retired from the Navy. Following the family tradition, Tom and Tim enlisted in the Navy when they were old enough. Thereafter, almost in unison, they took Viet Namese brides, divorced these brides after ten years, advanced to the rank of Chief, and retired after thirty years of service. Tim and Tom moved back to Pensacola, and now lived together in a small house off Via de Luna Drive on Pensacola Beach.

As fellow frequenters of Bobby D's, they became fast friends with Colonel Dubach and became part of the poker group. Tom and Tim didn't care much about high-rise development, but felt that whatever the Colonel said was right must be so.

*****

"Goddamn, boys. That operation was not up-to-snuff. A goddamn disaster, I'd say," rumbled the Colonel. "I'd say we performed like a bunch of boy scouts, but the scouts are a pretty good organization."

The militia was huddled in the den of the Colonel's home, Chou still panting after the night's escapade. Tom and Tim wore the look of a couple of coon hounds returning to their master after losing the scent.

"Well, damn, Colonel," Chou said defensively. "Who wudda thought thet ol' fart would be awake, much less catch us? An' you'd think even if he didn't have a flashlight, he wuddna stuck a match in the gas tank."

"Successful covert ops aren't built on assumptions. Never assume," snapped the Colonel.

Tom and Tim continued their hangdog.

"Well, as they say, if we don't hang together,

we will most certainly hang separately – manslaughter, at the least," opined the Colonel. "The question is, are we still intent on our purpose?" He eyed each man intently.

Tom and Tim spoke together, as usual. "We're still with you one hundred percent, Colonel. Whatever you say."

Chou thought momentarily, then replied, "Tha ol' man's death was unfortunate, but it doesn't erase the difficulty. If we don' stop this creepin' ovahdevelopment of ouah island, nobody else will, and the govament shur won't. Ah say we stay on track."

After a brief pause, the Colonel continued. "Good men. Now go home, and start thinking about our next move. I'll see you all Wednesday night, as usual."

CHAPTER 4

Jamar Abdula sat transfixed by the ocean, as he always was. As far as he could see, there was nothing but water. Could it be that this great salty mass never ended? And if it did, what did it end with? A cliff? A cliff that dropped off to what? More water? To nothing at all? How could that be? Perhaps that is where Allah lives sometimes, or always, he reasoned.

Of course, Abdula had heard the old fishermen talking of other lands where other people lived, but he did not believe them. If they were there, why could he not see them? No, he concluded, only Allah existed where he could not see. Other things were either seeable or they did not exist at all.

Abdula was not a stupid boy; he was sheltered. Abdula's world consisted of the tiny island of Sal, a small part of the Cape Verde Islands, off the coast of Africa at approximately 17° north latitude and 23° west longitude. Abdula, with the certainty of a ten-year-old boy, knew the things in his universe that were and the things that were not. Sal was the center of the universe, and it would be years before anyone could convince him otherwise.

Now Abdula was concerned with the mysteries of the universe, and the preeminent area of his focus was the transition taking place in the waters surrounding his home.

Abdula could not know that only miles to the north, the barometer was flirting with the one-thousand-millibar mark, cumulonimbus cloud formations towered beyond the imagination, even Abdula's, and the wind churned the ocean's waves toward staggering heights, as the entire system began a discernible counterclockwise movement.

What distressed Abdula was that the colors of his island paradise were being muted, turning ugly. The turquoise that normally faded to the color of the sky and then to navy was turning an angry cobalt gray. The golden sunshine had faded into a leaden overcast. These were, of course, things that Abdula had witnessed before in his short life, but these changes were somehow unique. He could even feel the difference in the air.

*****

Thousands of miles to the west – 33.45° north latitude; 84.23° west longitude – James Singer moved toward the Weather Channel camera to emphasize that he was serious.

"And good news for the Caribbean Sea and the Gulf of Mexico. For the time being all is quiet. But look here." He pointed at nothing in the studio, but on the air his finger traced along just south of the Tropic of Cancer. "We've got quite a disturbance. An amazing amount of convection just coming off the coast of Africa, and on our satellite image," he changed the on-screen image with a remote handswitch, "this is a monster. The cloud cover must run from the Cape Verdes to the Canaries. Wow! But, hey, there's a lot of water between this baby and any significant land. We'll keep an eye on it for you, though.

"For now," his tone changed along with the TV image, "how about Dallas?" Now he pointed to a bright red dot in the north central region of Texas. "One hundred and ten degrees, and it's September, folks. That bad little boy, *El Nino*, has sure upset the apple cart ... "

*****

Moving south – 30.19° north latitude;

87.09° west longitude – Charlie Cross sat in the cabin of his sloop, covered in grease and sweat. It had been some time since the oil had been changed in the diesel, mainly because Charlie hated doing it, and now was the time. Either that or risk ruining the whole engine.

Charlie knew if he'd been above board out on the gulf, where he wanted to be, he would have been enfolded in a gorgeous almost-fall day. As it was, he could only think about sticking his head up now and then for fear of dribbling gritty black oil on even more of the boat.

As Charlie pumped the last of the bad stuff into an old gallon milk carton, and began pouring the good stuff into the engine, he felt the boat rock. Why can't boaters learn to read? "NO WAKE ZONE" meant don't make a wake, as in: slow your ass down. The mental images of cigar boats or, worse yet, jet skis began to cloud Charlie's mind and deepen the frown that had already resulted from his dislike for the activity in which he was involved.

"Hi, sugah," came a female voice immediately over his head, followed by the smiling face of Tallulah Vidalia – "Lula" to the islanders.

Normally Charlie would have been glad to receive a pop-in visit from Lula, but because

Charlie was mentally elsewhere, this had the same effect as someone jumping out of a dark corner screaming "buga-buga!" The result was the involuntary release of the oil can, and a jump that ended in a loud bang as Charlie's bald spot met the bulkhead.

"Damn, Lula, you scared the shit outta me." Charlie rubbed his head and surveyed the spreading oil slick on the floor. At least it was a clean oil slick. "You need to give a guy a little notice 'fore you jump outta nowhere."

"Well, excuse me, Mr. Cross." Lula feigned offense. "I was just boiling some shrimp, and thought you might want to come by for dinner and ... whatever. But now, I don't know. You look like an ol' troll and you behave like one, too. A girl might do better elsewhere on the dock."

Charlie wasn't particularly hungry, but the "whatever" sounded promising. "Oh hell, Lula, I'm sorry. You just startled me. I was thinkin' about somethin' else, and this job has a tendency to make a person cranky, and it's hot down here, and it's a pretty day out there, and ... God forgive me. If you'll just give me another chance, I'll clean up my act, and even bring the beer. Give me another chance, eh? I scrub up real nice, and the likes of me could pleasure a lady like yourself." His whining drifted off into a bad English accent.

"I'm thinkin' I'm daft, but you'll get yer chance, you will. 'Alf five. Be there or be ... without." Lula vanished as quickly as she appeared.

Charlie unrolled a massive quantity of paper towel to create a dike to stop the spread of oil, then set about swabbing the glistening part of the lower deck. He recalled the first time he had noticed Lula.

Charlie had been happily drinking beer at the interior bar of Peg Leg Pete's.

He had long been familiar with the beach bar and eatery from occasional visits after his days in the Navy, but the place had expanded since then. Just as it had been during his first encounter, Peg Leg's had that look of something that had survived a hurricane or two: a structure on stilts whose wood had long since lost whatever color it originally had, if it ever did have a color. It had a weathered sun-bleached look which gave it instant credibility as a beach bar, perhaps even a Caribbean beach bar. Now, however, the proprietor had expanded the lower area to accommodate an additional outside bar and volleyball court. This latter addition was christened the "UnderWhere."

Charlie had been working on his boat in the sun all day, and as a consequence, had no desire to sit outside where the volleyballers played the game like true amateurs. Sweating with effort, coated with sand, they always looked like lightly battered pieces of red meat ready to be deep fried. Charlie had better things to do, one of which was to appreciate the pitcher of golden liquid that now sat half-empty before him.

Through the dull roar of conversation, loud music, and the thock-thock-ding-ding of a video game, Charlie's drifting and dreaming was halted by the raspy voice of some female apparently complaining mightily to the cashier.

"Listen, sugah, if ya'll keep puttin' posters and such on top of it, no one's evah gonna see it, much less buy it. Now how hard is that to remembah?"

The cashier, who must have been at least twenty-one, but looked more like seventeen, greeted this tirade with a mixture of awe and anger. Who was this woman, and just where did she get off telling me anything? The cashier's countenance was transparent.

The woman, as it turned out, was Tallulah Vidalia, and her little outburst had resulted from the inadvertent placement of a beach poster over Lula's latest shell creation, which Peg Leg's had agreed to market in the glass case beside the cash register.

Of course, Charlie didn't know that at the time. He had turned to recapture the relationship he had established with his beer, as each party took a more conciliatory posture and volume.

What Charlie had noticed was Lula's blonde-streaked hair, worn long and beachy around a well-tanned and attractively freckled face. The svelte body lightly camouflaged by the flowing shapeless dress had also gotten his attention. But it was the high cheek bones and flashing green eyes that really registered.

Now, to his right, Charlie sensed, rather than saw, a person taking the barstool beside him. Turning his head slightly, hoping it wasn't some fisherman or fat tourist, he noted with approval that his luck looked to be changing. His beer affair would have to wait.

"Hi! My name's Charlie," he said, with dazzling originality. This gambit was met with a bored stare. Not one to easily recognize the obvious, he continued, "I couldn't help but hear the ruckus over there. What was the deal?"

Charlie fought the pull of Lula's gold-flecked

green eyes by looking back at his jilted microbrew. To look too long would surely turn him into a pillar of salt, or a babbling fool. Sneaking a quick peek, Charlie saw that Lula's look had softened.

"Well, OK, Mistah Charlie. Name's Tallulah, but people call me Lula." She had the look of a person tasting something she knew she wouldn't like. "And for yoah information, the ruckus, as you put it, was because some people don't undastand maaketing. You see, Ah'm an aatist, and my medium is shayll. This fine establishment has agreed to display some of mah work, but it's hahd to call somethin' displayed when it's undah somethin' else. So Ah was merely pointin' that fact out to that cashier yonder."

Tallulah was a perfect name for this woman, Charlie mused. He offered to buy her a beer. Somehow this woman and a cold beer didn't seem to fit together, but, as far as he knew, Peg Leg's didn't have mint juleps.

Recognizing Charlie's hesitancy, Lula allowed as how "beah would be jus' fine. In fact, beah is one of mah very favorites."

Things progressed and Charlie learned that Lula had been born in Savannah, the only child of a doctor and his wife. Although Lula's parents channeled her in the direction of a university education where she might pledge a proper sorority and meet a proper husband, Lula had other ideas. After high school, she advised her parents that she needed to see some of the world before continuing her education, and headed for Europe with all the money she could garner and a backpack full of her worldly belongings.

Seeing "some of the world" turned out to be most of Europe, and ended in Dublin, Ireland, where she met a nice terrorist boy. His name was Seamus, and he was waging war on England generally, but specifically on Protestants in Northern Ireland. To young Lula, this seemed a most important cause, not to mention romantic, and she settled down to life as the woman of a freedom fighter.

Although Seamus never went into the details of his crusade, his work did necessitate his absence for extended periods of time. At first, love conquered all. But, after a while, Lula began to get damn sick of being without Seamus most of the time, only to be occasionally awakened in the middle of the night by a smelly old freedom fighter demanding sex.

It went without saying that Lula's parents were not happy. Dr. Vidalia bemoaned the fact that his daughter had now probably passed the age for what he considered a normal education, courtship, and marriage.

Meanwhile, Lula occupied herself in Dublin with various creative pursuits. Eliminating writing, music, painting, and acting, she finally found her niche in sculpture. Specifically, she found acceptance in modern art, involving the arrangement of odd items into forms of common experience.

Nevertheless, gluing stuff together was no substitute for love, companionship, and home. Fortunately, Seamus, always accommodating in a terroristic sort of way, contrived to cling a bit too long to a firebomb he had intended to hurl into a Protestant pub, and was conflagrated from this earth. Grieving only slightly, Lula headed for the good old U.S. of A.

After a brief honeymoon of reconciliation, Lula and her parents discovered they had grown apart. Lula had no intention of being dominated and directed by her parents, and Dr. and Mrs. Vidalia had no interest in housing a hippie artist.

Again fate intervened with death, this time of Lula's grandmother. With a nice inheritance, Lula said "see you later" to Savannah, and struck out for the promised land. This turned out to be Pensacola Beach.

What with the exchange of life stories, Charlie and Lula hadn't noticed they were being overserved, and, as a consequence, were not in the best of shape for lovemaking. Still, they tried, and with time and practice they improved.

These were the things that had occupied Charlie's thoughts this fine September day, as he finished the boat and cleaned up. Now he was headed for Lula's house with a twelve-pack tucked under his arm, and visions of boiled shrimp and Lula dancing through his head.

CHAPTER 5

Not everybody on the island was lost in the world of boys and girls and boat cleaning. The high sheriff of Escambia County sat in his office at the beach substation staring idly out at the Gulf of Mexico with his feet propped up on a government-issue credenza.

Slidell Goodbee had been sheriff ever since old Decker Phillips had retired, leaving Slidell his heir apparent. After a tough battle on his initial run for office, no one had ever challenged him again, and after seeing Slidell in action, not many ever wanted to. It wouldn't be an accurate statement to say that Sheriff Goodbee had brought law west of the Escambia River, but he had maintained Decker Phillips's high standards. Most voters were pleased with the job Slidell was doing, and would-be opponents still recalled the results of his first win. Not only had he beat the guy in the race for office, but also that same guy ended up with a bullet hole right in the middle of his forehead.

The death had been ruled a homicide, but no one had ever been brought to justice on that account. In fact, Slidell Goodbee had nothing to do with the murder, but the rumor mill began to darkly hint that the election and the death were connected, even though they were years apart. The idea of being defeated in an election and then eventually killed for good measure tended to keep folks out of Slidell's way, in politics and other areas of life. Realizing the advantage, Slidell didn't make an issue of the rumor being false; he just didn't address it at all.

With his hat pulled down on his forehead and his feet propped up, the casual observer might have mistaken Slidell's thinking position for napping. It was anything but. This was where and how Slidell liked to work things out in his head.

Unfortunately, it was taking a conscious effort to brush aside the little interoffice issue of someone using official phones to call "900" phone-sex numbers. It wasn't a big deal; it was just bothersome, like an itch in the middle of your back. If you ignored it, it would go away, but if you thought about it, it would drive you crazy.

By an act of will, then, he focused on the untimely death of Hulen Puckett. Although the *News Journal* had obliquely raised the specter of a murder on the beach, there just hadn't been any evidence to support that theory of death.

Sure the guy was dead and absent a head by violent means, but there was nothing to suggest that anybody was involved but Hulen Puckett. In fact, the burnt matches found scattered near the burned-out dozer strongly suggested that Puckett did himself, probably by accident.

So what? End of story. Case closed. And that could have been the end of it. But there were several issues that crossed Slidell's mind. The first was the death scene itself: the building site of a highly controversial, to say the least, high-rise condominium. Second, why the hell was Hulen lighting matches around an earthmoving machine – especially around the open gas tank? And why was the gas tank open in the first place?

The first two questions highlighted the third problem: if Slidell said it wasn't a homicide and more bodies started turning up, people – as in the electorate – would think the sheriff missed the ball. And a missed ball could be damned important if it meant more dead citizens.

One of Slidell's deputies had found Hulen's

flashlight, and, sure enough, it didn't work. But that could have been caused by the explosion. Furthermore, even if the flashlight hadn't been working before the explosion, why would a person be lighting matches in the middle of the night on the beach? One obvious answer, Slidell concluded, was to see something. Genius at work, he smiled sarcastically. But what could a person see with a match in an open field?

Shit, the matches could have been left there by kids hiding out and smoking dope. Maybe that's what Hulen was investigating. But then why would Hulen have a match in his hand? Trying out a doobie? Naw. Not old Hulen. He would've tried battery acid before he'd have smoked marijuana.

Slidell concluded that the only thing all this thinkin' was doin' was givin' him a headache. Maybe he'd just say the case was still under investigation, and leave it at that. At least, he'd do that if the press would leave him alone.

He watched as the sky began to turn a fiery pink. Slidell liked this time of year. Usually he couldn't see any part of a sunset from gulfside, but as the sun moved south for the winter, it would get better and better.

He stood, slamming his desk drawer, and resolved to think more about it later. Now, he might have just enough daylight to check out the crime scene one more time. Who knew, maybe the fading sunglow would cause a clue to jump out?

"Takin' it to the house, Sheriff?" said fat Atwood, the deputy handling the three-to-eleven shift, as Slidell headed out the door of the substation.

Although he couldn't be on duty all the time, Slidell hated it when his employees noted his leaving for the day. He thought about explaining to Atwood that he was still working on the Puckett case, but figured he'd just be wasting his breath. They'd think what they wanted to anyway.

"Supper's waitin' and I gotta get to it," he said instead, mocking the stereotype of the big-bellied rural sheriff. Atwood probably hadn't caught the humor. Slidell grimaced as he wheeled his unit east in the direction of Navarre.

Time was, Slidell mused as he passed Bobby D's and noted the locals beginning the evening ritual, he would be heading home about now, knowing his wife, Daphne, would be beginning to wonder where he was. Now she'd be at her office, trying to get her cases in order for the next day.

After he and Daphne had married, twins, a boy and a girl, had followed in short order.

Daphne had played the role of new mother very well for a while, a really short while. Then she began to tire of being a happy homemaker. During one of their increasingly frequent fights, she advised Slidell that she had no intention of becoming what she referred to as braindead. She enrolled at the University of West Florida to finish her degree.

At first, this new development caused Slidell some distress; he wasn't used to sharing Daphne. Now the kids and school claimed a good bit of her time. However, he noted that his wife seemed happier, and the frequency of their fights decreased to a tiff now and again. This would work, he had concluded, and he had been quite proud when Daphne graduated.

The real surprise came when she announced that she had been accepted at the University of Florida School of Law's satellite night school in Pensacola. But, reasoning that law school was better than having her playing around out of boredom, he resolved to muddle through with a part-time wife and mother.

Really, though, it hadn't been that bad so far, except around finals time. He found the extra effort on his part was mightily appreciated by Daphne, and he got close to the kids at a time in their lives when most other kids were pretty much the exclusive province of moms.

But now Daphne had declared criminal law as her field of choice, and, what was worse, Slidell didn't even get until graduation from law school for that to soak in. She had enrolled in a sort of practicum in which she would actually practice criminal law, beginning this semester under the tutelage of an experienced criminal defense lawyer.

Now, as Slidell kicked through the scorched area where the dozer had been, he wasn't exactly focused on the hunt. Slidell was thinking he would just have to get used to having a criminal lawyer for a wife, either that or find something better. But the latter wasn't really an option, since he'd never been even remotely attracted to anyone else but Daphne. But still, living with a defense lawyer? He winced, showing his puzzle wrinkles, and headed back toward his car.

Just as he moved from the scorched ring of earth, the last rays of the day caused something to gleam momentarily. Assuming the only thing likely to be shiny out here was a twist-off cap, he almost ignored it. But recalling that he was out here to look for clues, closer examination proved that the item was not a bottle cap at all, but a small silver replica of something that resembled a hamburger. It had a small hole in it, suggesting the sort of thing that a person might wear on a chain around their neck.

A hamburger? It probably wasn't related to Puckett's death, but it was curious just the same. Why would anybody make such a thing, and, if someone did, who would want it?

CHAPTER 6

The sea breeze was coming due south over the island at about ten knots, gently pushing the boat through the cut connecting LaFitte Cove with Santa Rosa Sound. Charlie cut hard to starboard and came up into the wind. Lula hoisted the mainsail and unfurled the jib sail. Charlie then steered hard a port, shut down the diesel – which now had clean oil – and the sloop fell off on a beam reach as the sails filled.

Charlie always felt this particular maneuver, although not difficult at all, was as graceful and satisfying as any of the precision flying conducted by the Blue Angels. He knew he might get an argument on that point from most Pensacolians, but he guessed sailors might agree. The almost total synchronicity with natural forces and the sleek lines of the vessel gave him the feeling of tapping into, and becoming part of, the basic rhythm of the planet.

Charlie donned his symbol of command, a

blue gimmie cap stenciled *The Blues*, and addressed his crew. "A beer for the captain, and likewise for his mate."

Lula looked askance.

"OK. Could I please have a beer?" Charlie said.

Lula complied and took a seat next to Charlie on the transom, as the sun, now a massive crimson wafer, began its rapid slide through Perdido Key.

The plan had been to repay Lula for the dinner she had cooked the other night by taking her out on the boat for a quick cruise east to Quietwater Beach and a meal somewhere along the Boardwalk. Usually, at this time of year, it was easy enough to dodge the Hobie Cats as they raced helter-skelter around the sound and to dock at the Quietwater pier. So far the whole thing had gone off without a hitch, leaving the sloop neatly tucked between two mammoth yachts.

Because the night was warm, the Boardwalk was fairly crowded. Someone was celebrating a wedding at Jubilee's, the younger set jammed into the new Bamboo Willie's, and Sun Ray's was taking names for seating. It wasn't exactly what Charlie had hoped for, so they decided to pick up a couple of burgers at Memory Station and head back to the boat. It wasn't grilled mahi-mahi, but the burgers were always good, and Charlie had stowed a fair quantity of cold beer in the hold of the *Long Gone*.

As it turned out, this was an excellent alternative. The air cooled as the almost-full moon rose, and Steve Gunter rocked the night with Delta blues from the band shell.

Sometime around the witching hour, the music stopped. They could have headed back for LaFitte Cove, but it was one of those enchanted evenings when the moon turned the sound to silver. So, by mutual consent, they turned the boat east. The relative calm of the sound allowed Charlie to engage the autopilot, and off they sailed in the moonlight, accompanied by the romantic sounds of Willie Nelson's *Stardust* on the CD player.

As they snuggled close to ward off the night chill, Charlie was a happy man. The elements of contentment were his: the music of love, a fine boat under sail in the moonlight, a beautiful lady curled around him, and four black-clad figures creeping around the new construction site of the Sandcastle Beach Hotel and Condominiums.

*****

Hours earlier, the Wooliebooger Militia had convened at the house of the Colonel. Tim Riley was speaking for the two brothers, as usual.

"Tommy and I looked the place over yesterday. They've got a new security guard, but he's even worse than the other one. He's a fat guy from New York, and his idea of night security is a place to sleep after his day job. He comes in, makes his rounds, and nighty-night 'til the sun rises."

"Thet's what we thought about tha otha guy, and look what happened," cautioned Chou. "Maybe we should check on this new guy faw a couple aw weeks to make shur of his routine."

"We could check forever, Chou," Tom chimed in, "and, sure as hell, on the night we'd pick for the op, he'd get an attack of conscience and patrol all night long. Besides that, this little caper will happen about as far from the guard shack as you can get and still be on Sandcastle property."

"Thet's jus' fine to say, Tom, but you may recall ouah last little capah was supposed to be a piece o' cake also. Thet ended up with a mudah, and you lost yoah goddamn medal."

The medal had been Tom and Tim's idea. They had convinced the Colonel that any covert military unit worth its salt needed a symbol, like a beret or something. And since they couldn't be real obvious about their activities, Tim had suggested a medal of some sort that could be taken off when they weren't on "official business." The Colonel, being a retired military man himself and therefore having respect for the power of symbols, had OKed the plan, and left it to Tom and Tim to find the proper symbol. This turned out to be more difficult than the brothers had suspected, and the closest they could get to a "Wooliebooger" was the little Superburger pins in the shape of a hamburger that the local Superburger Drive-In in Gulf Breeze used for promotions.

As Tom was about to protest Chou's accusative manner, the Colonel intervened. "Gentlemen. Gentlemen. No need to get excited. These things happen. Why, look at the Normandy invasion."

Tom, Tim, and Chou weren't old enough to remember the SNAFUs that happened on D-Day, but they'd seen the movies, so they nodded.

"What we need to do now is focus on the current operation so nothing will go wrong this time." The Colonel paused to allow the team to collect themselves. "Tom, it was your idea, you lay it out for us."

Tom moved off in the direction of the

Colonel's dining room table, where they had constructed a mock-up of the Sandcastle Beach Hotel and Condominiums construction site as well as the Santa Rosa Sound as far west as the Colonel's home. This was one of Tom's favorite parts, and he began as he supposed a real commando would.

"At twenty-four-hundred hours, we will disembark from base camp ..."

"You mean the Colonel's house, Tom," Chou interrupted. All this military stuff was fine, but there was a game aspect here that seemed dangerous. They weren't playing army here.

Tom bristled, but again the Colonel interceded. "It's Tom's op plan. Let him explain it the way he wants to."

Chou shrugged and looked away.

"At twenty-four-hundred hours, we will disembark from base camp." Tom emphasized the last two words for Chou's benefit. "Then we will proceed east by water in full covert gear. At zero-zero-thirty-hours, we arrive at ground zero and deploy."

Chou rolled his eyes, but didn't say anything.

"The Colonel then proceeds to this area," Tom pointed to a position near the guard shack, "and acts as lookout. Tim moves to this location,"

Tom pointed again, "and secures the hydrant control. I secure the hose, and move to the target. On my order, Tim engages the water mechanism."

"What about me, Tom?" Chou queried.

"You stay between me and Tim to relay my instructions to Tim. Then, after disabling the construction materials, at exactly zero-one-hundred hours, we rendezvous at the disembarkment vessel and execute a controlled evacuation of the target zone. Oh yeah, here, each of you take one of these." Tom handed each of the team a small flashlight that looked like it was won from a gumball machine.

Chou wondered how many quarters this had cost Tom.

"One flash answered by one flash means everything is OK," Tom continued. "Two flashes mean halt operations and maintain silence. Three flashes mean we've been detected, and a controlled rapid departure should be executed forthwith. Any questions?"

The Colonel stood staring at the mock-up with his hand covering his mouth and chin, a contemplative posture that Chou would have bet was an attempt to mask a snigger.

Chou spoke first. "Tom, does thet mean wea gonna hose down the cement?"

"You know that's what it means, Chou. That stuff is quick dry, and by the time they get around to needin' it, they'll have a humagiferous hunk of concrete block that ain't good for nothin'."

The Colonel gestured for silence. "Sounds like a good plan to me, Tom. Now we've got a little time before we go, so you gentlemen silently run through this in your minds, and make sure you and your gear are in order. And one other thing. Don't wear your medals tonight. Damn things come off too easy."

*****

Charlie sat staring at the incongruity, not quite believing what he saw. "Do you believe that?"

"What I believe is you'ah not much of a date for a passionate young lady," answered Lula. "Just sittin' there lookin' like you ate somethin' bad."

"No. No. Look over there," Charlie pointed excitedly.

Lula obliged. "Whatever are those men doin'?"

"Hard to tell from here, but I don't think they're part of the construction crew," answered Charlie, recalling the death of the security guard and the four strangers. He switched off the autopilot and heaved to. "I'll be right back," he promised, as he made for the cabin.

Snatching the hand mike for the radio, he broadcast "*Securite, Securite,*" the distress hailing for third level emergencies on the water. He didn't know whether *securite* was quite right, but *mayday* and *pan-pan* were a bit too strong for something that wasn't life threatening or imminent. He didn't know what the right call was actually – he figured Chapman's *Piloting* hadn't envisioned this type of emergency – but he needed attention quick.

"*Securite, Securite,*" he hailed again. "This is sailing vessel *Long Gone* at 87° west longitude, 30.2° north latitude, seeking Coast Guard assistance. Unidentified intruders in the area of the Sandcastle Beach Hotel up to no good." Up to no good, he grimaced. What kind of distress hailing is that?

Somebody else apparently had the same thought; they almost immediately came back with "Git off the goddamned radio. This ain't no police frequency."

What a charming person, Charlie thought, fighting off the impulse to respond in kind. However, this sort of stuff wasn't uncommon. Put a radio transmitter in some people's hands and they became the self-appointed monitor of the air waves.

As Charlie was about to transmit again, despite his on-air critics, the radio came alive. "Vessel *Long Gone*, this is the Coast Guard. Sir, this doesn't sound like a Coast Guard matter, but we've patched your message through to the Escambia County Sheriff."

"That's a roger and thanks," responded Charlie.

"Told ya so," said the asshole.

With that taken care of, Charlie returned topside to find Lula peering intently at the activity on the shore.

Apparently, the sheriff had been faster than Charlie had thought possible. Either that or the black-clad figures had completed whatever they were doing, for they moved in unison toward what Charlie now recognized as a boat and cast off.

Charlie didn't know whether the little group was going after him or just going, but he didn't think it was a good idea to hang around to see. Shifting the jib appropriately, he brought the *Long Gone* about seventy-five degrees and headed off in the direction of Gulf Breeze. Just for good measure, he cranked the diesel up to two thousand rpms. He hoped the intruders didn't have a big engine on their boat, just in case they intended to chase him.

*****

The deputy hadn't been far away when he got the call from the dispatcher advising of the Coast Guard communication. However, when the deputy arrived at the Sandcastle site, all was quiet. In fact, he had to waken the fat security guard. They walked the area, but found nothing suspicious. Water on the beach didn't really seem out of place.

"Must have been a prank," the deputy shrugged, leaving the security guard to his sleeping.

CHAPTER 7

On the TV, some whiny oldster stopped carping about Medicare and smiled with obvious relief upon discovering God's gift to the AARP set – Golden Years Patriotic and Protective Assurance Company had apparently just come out with a policy to forever ward off the evils of a government conspiracy to increase the price of medical care beyond the range of those on fixed incomes. As the commercial faded on grampa's smiling face nuzzling his silver-haired mate, a new image materialized: Jordan Faith.

Jordan Faith also had a mane of silver and a face formed by craggy character wrinkles. Jordan Faith was a man you could trust. Conspicuously absent was James Singer, who had been detailing the ugly weather on the west coast just before the last round of commercials.

To the knowledgeable Weather Channeler, this could only mean one thing – that little disturbance in the Atlantic Ocean was about to be more disturbing. Jordan Faith only made an appearance when things were about to get bad.

"Hurricane hunters have now determined that there are sustained winds of eighty-five miles an hour in Hurricane Jorge. Yes, you heard me correctly, Hurricane Jorge.

"Until ten o'clock this morning, now-Hurricane Jorge was just a mass of convection spreading some one-hundred-and-fifty miles from both sides of the Tropic of Cancer. However, Jorge has now come together. If this storm continues to strengthen with this rapidity, it could be the storm of the century."

Jordan Faith was not a bullshitter. For anyone tuned to the Weather Channel living on the Atlantic Seaboard, the Caribbean Sea, or the Gulf of Mexico, Faith's statement caused an involuntary tightening of the abdominal muscles.

"Hurricane Jorge is currently at longitude 40° west and latitude 23.5° north, moving at a speed of twenty knots, due west. On the satellite picture, you can see the formation of a clearly defined eyewall." He pointed with a laser pen.

"It's a bit too early to forecast landfall. Steering currents could take this storm up and back out into the North Atlantic. Just the same, residents of the East Coast and the Caribbean should keep an eye out. Of course, you can tune in here at the Weather Channel. We'll be watching Jorge for you. Now James Singer's going to tell you what's keeping Texas so dry."

*****

After the first couple of days, Charlie had about chalked up the incident at the Sandcastle to one of those things that happen in life that you wonder about mightily at the time, but for which you never get an explanation. Now he was on step two or three of his morning ritual, drinking chocolate milk and reading the *News Journal* at a table in the UnderWhere. Scanning the "Local" section, an article on the progress of the Sandcastle development caught his eye:

> Questioned about the progress of the newest and largest high-rise development on Pensacola Beach, Leefert Davis, chief contractor for the operation, said things were "coming along nicely." In fact, he expressed pleasure that, despite minor problems with vandalism, they were already putting up the superstructure.
>
> Davis noted that vandals had apparently soaked much of the operation's concrete supply, rendering it useless. However, "in an outfit this size, we can get that

> ...(concrete) ... on a day's notice."
> Asked about a completion date ....

Charlie's mind wandered. So that's what the black-clad figures had been doing. Kinda funny for grown men – he supposed they were grown men; they looked like adults anyway – to be playing kids' tricks. Tuning back in to the article:

> Police reports from the Escambia County Sheriff's Department indicate a call was received two nights prior to the discovery of the damage, but nothing unusual was discovered at the time. Oddly enough, the call came through the Coast Guard, relayed by a concerned boater and island local, Charles Cross.

This addition, seemingly an afterthought by the reporter, caused Charlie to spit chocolate milk over the remainder of the paper. Charlie was not at all pleased that he had been identified as the informant.

*****

A couple of miles east, this same article was drawing interest from other concerned citizens. Ruston Dubach and Tim and Tom Riley sat eating cheese grits and fried eggs at Chan's Market while perusing the newspaper.

"Hmmm," intoned the Colonel, "looks like our little party wasn't very successful." He handed Tim the "Local" section.

Minutes later, while Tom was trying to digest the article as well, Tim responded, "That, an' we got us a snitch."

"Perhaps we've underestimated the opposition, and some adjustments are in order. But this isn't the time or the place." The Colonel glanced around the crowded diner. "Do you think Chou might be interested in an off-night poker game?"

Tim and Tom nodded as they finished off their breakfast and made ready to leave.

The men filed into Colonel Dubach's home at precisely seven-thirty that evening, carting six-packs of beer and bags of chips, as usual. They all sat at the dining room table, as usual. And left the drapes open, as usual. There were even cards, poker chips, and open beers on the table, as usual. To the casual observer or neighbor, this was just another poker game, just on a different night. What the unpracticed eye would not take in was that the men weren't actually eating, drinking, or doing anything but holding the cards while they talked in earnest.

"Gentlemen," intoned the Colonel, bringing the meeting to order, "it is my considered opinion that we have, to this point, been playing with ourselves. Not only is our target unaware that we even exist, but we are so feared that a local beach bum turns us in to the authorities, as if we were errant schoolboys. Are we in agreement on this? I would like to hear your opinions."

Tim leaped into the breach. "Colonel, I told you from the start. We should hit 'em hard so they'd by God feel it. It was Chou who wanted to play around."

Chou looked sideways across the table, controlling his impulse to say "Fuck you, Tim." Instead he said, "Ah nevah said we should play aroun', Tim. Mah only suggestion was thet we go slow. Ease into it. Obviously, Ah undahestimated the size of ouah opposition. An elephant don' care much when a flea bites him on the ass. Clearly, stronger measures ah called fah."

"I think Tim's right," Tom chimed in. "We need to kick a little butt."

Surprise, surprise, thought Chou.

After a pause for effect, Colonel Dubach continued. "Then we're all in agreement. Stronger measures are called for. But what measures do you suggest?" Some leaders simply tell their followers what to do. Colonel Dubach liked to let his men think they were making the decisions.

"I think we ought to blow the damn thing up," blurted Tim, a model of aggressive self-assurance.

"Thet's nice, Tim," said Chou softly. "But what is it exac'ly thet you think we should blow up?"

"Well, the ...," Tim started, then realized there wasn't anything to blow up. They had just started on the superstructure. Crestfallen, Tim said nothing more.

Tom followed suit for a brief period, then seemed to recall the other difficulty.

"We still got that snitch to deal with. We gotta show people there's a price for rattin' us out."

"An' which one of us is it thet is goin' to wield the bloody knife?" queried Chou, mostly rhetorically.

"I didn't say nothin' about killin'. There's other things that'll get a person's attention," retorted Tom. "Just leave the snitch to Tim and me."

Colonel Dubach wasn't too happy with the idea of leaving anything solely to Tom and Tim.

They hadn't done so well with the medal thing, and by all indications, rocket science was not their hobby.

But to take the matter out of their hands at this point would run contrary to his style of leadership. It was a gamble, but they did seem to have a certain "street-smart."

"OK, that seems a good course of action. This plan of yours, Tom, isn't anything that will imperil our primary goal, is it?" The Colonel peered over his reading glasses suspiciously.

"Naw. Me and Tim done it before. Just shakes 'em up good. Let's 'em know you're out there and you're serious," reassured Tim.

That seemed to satisfy the Colonel.

Chou was not reassured at all.

"Now, to the matter of our primary target," the Colonel continued. "You seem to be saying we should strike a death blow to the building. Yet there is not enough building to deal with. Let me suggest we lay low awhile, allow the construction to continue. Then we detonate an explosive, and let them know that war has been declared." He sat back, waiting for the reaction.

The three men nodded their assent.

The Colonel concluded with a suggestion that they meet at a later date to further discuss both the resolution of the informant and more concrete action plans.

CHAPTER 8

The chocolate milk had long since evaporated, along with the anxiety Charlie had originally felt at being labeled as an informant in the newspaper. As he made his way across Fort Pickens Road, he took care to look long and hard east and west on the darkened beach highway. Although it was "late in the evening" – the Paul Simon tune rang in his slightly foggy head – there was no telling when a drunken beach reveler might come weaving home from a party somewhere or other.

The night had gone very well. Very well, Charlie nodded, smiling slightly. Charlie wished he hadn't had to go back to his boat, but Lula was expecting clients early the next morning, and Charlie was supposed to have an engine ready for use the next day. In the fashion of the beach, schedules were kind of rough guidelines rather than something fixed in time. But now the owner had called to say that he would be at the marina in the late morning with a fishing party, and the boat didn't quite run yet.

Lula's grilled amberjack had been superb, as usual, and so was Lula. Dressed in what Charlie took to be a "beach cover," the contours of Lula's body were revealed every time she moved. After dinner, they finished their wine with the full moon reflecting on the gulf, and nature took its course – several times. The lingering kiss on Lula's front porch finished the perfect evening, and now Charlie looked forward to sweet dreams as his boat bobbed gently in the balmy night air.

Coming through the parking lot at Peg Leg's, Charlie's first clue that all was not well was the black-and-white deputy sheriff's cruiser blocking the walkway to the boat ramp. Charlie understood that now and again deputies investigated complaints at LaFitte Cove Marina, but he wasn't quite prepared to see a fat Deputy Atwood rummaging through the *Long Gone* with a flashlight.

"Excuse me," Charlie hollered, as he approached his boat. He had wanted to say "What the hell are you doing on my boat, you fat asshole?" but he figured that might get things off on the wrong foot.

"Well, now." Atwood raised his bulk from the

cabin floor and smiled at Charlie. "Looks like I got me a perp."

Charlie understood that "perp" was cop-ese for the perpetrator of a crime, and the label as applied to him was not thrilling.

"What do you mean, perp, Deputy?" Charlie inquired, as respectfully as the situation allowed.

"Hold it right there, boy," directed the deputy, making his way toward the dock and Charlie. For a moment it looked like Atwood would tilt and fall into the sea, but, unfortunately, he didn't. In short order, he was on Charlie, spinning him toward the trash receptacle.

"Assume the position," barked Atwood.

"What the hell are you talking about? What's going on?" Charlie had now lost patience. This was not good.

"Son, don't resist," Atwood warned, with a slight sneer and assuming a stance that portended violence.

Charlie thought, you fuckin' idiot, but said, "OK. OK. Take it easy. What do you want me to do?"

For a moment, it could have gone either way, but Atwood seemed to compose himself, finally saying, "That's better. Now put your hands on the trash can."

Charlie complied, and Atwood quickly frisked him, then handcuffed Charlie's wrists behind his back.

"Now you kneel down right there, and don't move 'til I'm finished here."

Charlie had little choice; he did as he was told.

Charlie was relieved that the beach bar was closed and the houses around the cove were dark. Merely being the subject of police action was embarrassing enough without the added indignity of kneeling handcuffed on the dock. Finally, Atwood emerged from the *Long Gone*, smiling in Charlie's direction. In his raised right hand, he was waving something in a clear cellophane container.

"Well, now, Mr. Charlie, I think this will do the trick." He smirked.

Charlie knew he had some lunch meat packaged in cellophane, but he couldn't imagine that lunch meat would excite anybody, even fat Atwood.

"What's the problem, Deputy? Is there something wrong with keeping lunch meat on a boat?" Charlie realized that something wasn't what it appeared.

"No. Unless it's crushed white lunch meat, and you eat it through a straw in your nose,"

Atwood wisecracked. "But I think the lab boys'll find that this here ain't lunch meat at all. I think they'll find it's candy, nose candy."

Even when Atwood got next to him, Charlie couldn't see exactly what he was holding. But Atwood put whatever it was in his left shirt pocket, and from his right shirt pocket he extracted a small laminated card with large print on it.

"Charles Travis Cross, I'm arresting you for the offense of possessing a usable quantity of a controlled substance, to wit: cocaine."

A shock of disbelief reverberated through Charlie.

"You have the right to remain silent." Atwood was reading his card. "Anything you say can and will be used against you in a court of law. You have the right to an attorney, and if you can't afford one, the court will appoint one for you. Do you understand these rights?"

Charlie nodded lamely.

"OK, then, you wanna give 'em up, and tell me why you did it?"

Right, Atwood, thought Charlie, why don't I do that, and, as long as we're at it, why don't we skip the rest of the bullshit and go straight on down to Starke? But Charlie didn't say that; instead he said, "Before I say anything, I want a lawyer."

This caused Atwood to huff, and, stuffing the card back into his pocket, he roughly pulled Charlie to his feet and dragged him off in the direction of the patrol car.

"Suit yourself, hardcase," muttered Atwood, as they walked away, "but things might go easier if you 'fessed up."

Again the word "bullshit" echoed in Charlie's head.

Charlie had never been arrested before, but things went pretty much like he'd seen on TV. At least, they did until Atwood failed to turn the cruiser into the beach substation. This caused Charlie distress. He'd heard about bad cops beating a confession out of prisoners.

"Hey, deputy, where are we going? Isn't that the station right there?"

"Humpf," breathed Atwood, "and they said you used to be a lawyer."

Charlie didn't quite know how to interpret that remark. He learned later that Atwood thought the status of having been a lawyer automatically made a person aware that people arrested on the beach didn't go to the substation. Everybody arrested on Pensacola Beach went to the county jail in Pensacola proper.

Although Charlie had envisioned a nice quiet cell at the beach, maybe shared with a drunk teenager, he was still momentarily relieved when the deputy's cruiser finally pulled up to the county jail on North L Street downtown. That beat the devil out of what his worst fears had been.

Notwithstanding that he was apparently finally in the justice system, instead of in the clutches of some rogue cop, Charlie was scared. Although it was true that he was a lawyer, at least he was if his bar card hadn't expired, big firm probate types didn't make jail calls to help inmates make out their wills. Nobody had been mean to him, depending on how you classified Atwood's behavior, but folks at the jail weren't friendly. Coldly efficient was the term that came to mind.

Once they were inside, Atwood, to his credit, took off the handcuffs. That was immediately better. Then for some reason, Atwood required Charlie to assume the position and frisked him once again. Just routine, he supposed. Charlie was instructed to give an intake officer all his personal belongings, along with his belt and shoes. That was OK, too; he guessed some of those things could be used as a weapon or to commit suicide. But things were about to get worse.

Charlie was led back toward the front

entrance into a small room where he was photographed, front and side view, and then fingerprinted. The whole procedure had a numbing effect as he realized that he would now have a criminal record, complete with mug shots and fingerprints.

He knew he wasn't guilty of anything, but he also knew that even if he proved himself so, there would always be a record of his arrest – something police officers would see if they pulled him up on their computer, even as a result of something as simple as a speeding ticket. He was now a member of the "bad guys club" as far as law enforcement was concerned. If he ever chose to get a real job again, this would always be something he would have to explain. A question mark would always hang over his head in the eyes of legitimate society.

Had Charlie been a weaker man, or a drunker man, or even a younger man, he might have choked up as the reality of his new status sank in. But now he had other things to worry about. The intake officer was moving him in the direction of what he assumed was his cell. As they walked down a long corridor, he understood why this place was nicknamed "the slammer." Steel jail doors did not close with an electronic swoosh like the ones at the airport. His thoughts immediately turned to getting out of this place.

"When do I get my phone call, Deputy?" Charlie would have said "deputy sir," if he thought it would help.

"You'll get your turn," monotoned the deputy, as he opened the cell door with a large metal key.

If Charlie had thought the doors slamming before were loud, it was nothing to the sound of his own cell door clanging shut. He surveyed his new accommodations. This was not a private room with a bath. This was a "tank," a group housing unit for those awaiting release or more permanent placement.

Fortunately, it was late; most of his new roomies were asleep. Some were not, however, and they eyed Charlie as a snake might eye a field mouse. One of his new associates was a large hairy tattooed gentleman, who was now moving toward Charlie.

"Whacha in for, Dude?" growled the man.

Charlie thought, then responded, "Dope, but it wasn't mine."

The large ugly man snorted. "Another innocent citizen accused."

Charlie let that go by, trying to ignore his new friend.

"You got a woman on the outside?" Big Ugly

said.

Charlie hesitated, thinking that if he didn't answer, the guy would probably get pissed. "Yeah, I guess."

"You ever had a man?"

Cold fear ran through Charlie. He had heard stories about this kind of thing. He didn't know what to do. The man moved closer to him. There was no place to run. He'd have to fight.

As Big Ugly reached out for him, Charlie blocked him with his forearm and spun inside the man's grasp. He wasn't trying to cuddle up – he let his spin continue, trying to connect his other elbow with Big Ugly's jaw as forcefully as possible.

Big Ugly apparently had had experience with this sort of thing, because he merely grabbed the elbow and held Charlie with both arms, clapping a huge hairy hand over Charlie's mouth.

The man was a gorilla. Charlie couldn't move. Worse yet, the man was dragging Charlie over to the toilet area which blocked the visual from the detention officers, and a couple of Big Ugly's friends were coming over to get in on the party. As one of the new arrivals fumbled with Charlie's pants snap, Charlie heard the key inserted in the cell door's massive lock.

"Cross! Listen up. Your lawyer's here. Come

on." The bored detention officer directed him out.

Charlie could have hugged the officer. His other new friends released their hold on him, and he lurched out of the head and out of harm's way.

Big Ugly blew him a kiss, saying, "Too bad. Maybe next time."

CHAPTER 9

Charlie was sure that there had been some mistake. He didn't have a lawyer; even if he had had one, the lawyer wouldn't have known Charlie was in jail. So it was with the mindset of one tiptoeing past a guard dog late at night that Charlie went through the bookout procedure.

"You Charles Travis Cross?" asked the detention officer.

Charlie hesitated. What if he was looking for someone else? But since it would have been impossible to guess who that other person might be, he answered in the affirmative. Lord, don't let this be a mistake, he prayed.

"This your stuff?" the officer shoved a plastic bag at Charlie with what looked like his stuff in it.

"Yes, sir. That's it. Can't say it's been nice, but thanks anyway. I'll just be going now." Charlie knew he was rattling idiotically.

"Hold it!" ordered the officer.

The silence was electric. Charlie cringed and

held his breath.

"You gotta check it first. Don't want you claimin' we stole your stuff while you was our guest." The officer grinned sardonically.

Charlie checked everything as quickly as he could, again said some foolish good-bye, and strode off in the direction of freedom.

"Hold it! Where do you think you're going?"

Charlie stopped dead. This is the part where the officer will say there's been a mistake.

"Out?" Charlie grinned hopefully.

The officer eyed Charlie suspiciously, then pointed. "Out's the other way. That's where ya' jus' been."

Charlie burst through the door to the sallyport, not bothering to put on his shoes and belt. He was free and he didn't care if he was barefooted and beltless.

Looking around, Charlie saw the first rays of sunrise over the trees east of North H Street, and realized he would have to walk or hitchhike home. That was just fine with Charlie.

Deciding that shoes were going to be a necessity, he was busily toeing his flip-flops when a red Porsche pulled up beside him. Charlie didn't pay much attention, not knowing anyone who owned a Porsche, until he heard a female voice coming from within.

"Want a ride?"

Had he been much younger, Charlie would have marveled at his good fortune: a good looking woman in a sports car stopping to pick him up. No, he thought, no. This was another mistake. Bending down, Charlie peered in the open window, pointed at himself, and mouthed the word "me?"

"Yeah. You." The woman was laughing.

This was most peculiar to Charlie, but he was tired and did not really want to walk home. Furthermore, he knew that to refuse such an offer would cause him many sleepless nights thinking of what might have been.

"Thanks," he chirped, and hopped in.

As the driver went through the gears, then slowed and turned south on I-110, Charlie watched and wondered. This woman was pretty much drop-dead gorgeous and apparently wealthy. Why would she pick up a rumpled beach bum outside the county jail? That was what he wanted to ask, but he waited. This was her play.

She accelerated through the overpass curve and across Gregory Street toward the Three Mile Bridge over Pensacola Bay. No words were exchanged. Finally, shifting into fourth gear after the light, she glanced at Charlie.

"You're Charlie Cross."

Yes, that was true, he thought, but didn't say; he just waited.

"I'm Daphne Fairhope. I'm your lawyer."

This made a lot more sense than what Charlie had been fantasizing, but he said matter-of-factly, "I don't have a lawyer."

"Well, I know you didn't know you had a lawyer, but you do. Well, kind of a lawyer. What I mean is, I'm a law student in the criminal clinic, but I practice under a licensed attorney who specializes in criminal law. With me, it's kind of like having a lawyer-and-a-half representing you. I don't do anything without clearing it with Mr. Norton – he's my advisor – and when we go to court, Mr. Norton will handle that. I'll just assist him then. Of course, now that you're out, I don't have to be your lawyer anymore. You may choose to hire someone else. However, I would recommend you retain counsel," she explained, in what Charlie viewed as a very professional manner.

"Who retained you?" inquired Charlie, thinking that Daphne Fairhope might be some kind of flake.

"Oh, but of course, you couldn't know," she paused, apparently realizing the various things Charlie could have been thinking. Then, with a half-smile, and a twinkle in her eye, she explained. "Lula. She said she saw you being taken away in handcuffs last night and figured you'd need an attorney. So she called me. We've known each other since Lula got to the island. I've bought some of her art work."

Charlie expressed his gratitude and almost told her about his jail experience, but thought better of it. Charlie realized he didn't know any lawyers in the area, and Daphne said she practiced criminal law exclusively, so Charlie asked what the services of a lawyer-and-a-half would cost.

"Well, that's the good part." Daphne hesitated, hoping she hadn't insulted her client. "We don't charge much. It's on a sliding scale based on what the client can afford."

Charlie had heard of William Norton. He had a good reputation for walking anyone who could afford his fees. On the other hand, this woman was a law student. But then again, how much harm could she do on William Norton's tight leash? Besides that, the price was definitely right. Charlie didn't have any real money, so he guessed it wouldn't cost him much. All in all, it was a pretty good deal.

So it came to be that Daphne Fairhope, who, Charlie would later learn, was the wife of the county sheriff, represented Charlie Cross.

Charlie began to explain to Daphne what had happened the night previous, that he had no idea what Deputy Atwood had found or how it got there, or, for that matter, why Atwood was looking in his boat.

Daphne merely nodded, and said she would find out and get back to him. In the meantime, he was not to worry.

By this time, they were moving past the Dunes Hotel on the beach, and Charlie elected to be dropped at the Tom Thumb, as opposed to home. Chocolate milk sounded pretty good.

As the day warmed rapidly, Charlie sat in his usual place in the UnderWhere sipping his chocolate milk and trying to think. Not only was he tired, but his focus kept getting sidetracked by visions of Big Ugly.

Charlie knew the cocaine Atwood had found was not his. He didn't do cocaine, and he certainly didn't keep it around for guests. Given that, there seemed to be only two possibilities. Someone had been on his boat and dropped the drugs, either by accident or on purpose. Accidentally dropping drugs didn't seem very likely; if that had been the case, a person would not call the sheriff to help find them. Although Charlie hated these either-or conclusions, the only other possibility was that someone had planted the drugs and then alerted the police.

As Charlie began to compile a list of people who might truly hate him, reality intervened like a thump on the forehead. He had forgotten about the boat motor that had to be ready this morning. And using the I-got-busted-for-drugs-last-night-but-they-weren't-really-mine excuse didn't seem viable. So up he jumped and off he scurried in the direction of the *Long Gone* for tools. The long term, more serious problem would just have to wait. Getting dollars for his daily needs was more pressing.

CHAPTER 10

Although it wasn't quite time yet, Colonel Ruston Dubach believed in being prepared. It wouldn't do to give the "go" signal to the next step in their crusade, only to find out that they couldn't get the proper explosives. Tom and Tim claimed some expertise in demolitions, but the Colonel's evaluation of their level of competence dictated that he rely on his own experience for this part of the operation.

He knew what they needed, of course: plastic explosives, detonators, and timers. The problem had always been where to get such things without winding up in federal prison.

The Colonel had resolved that difficulty by contacting a former subordinate, who, prior to a dishonorable discharge, had been assigned to seek out enemy installations in Viet Nam and blow them up. Unfortunately, some left-leaning Congress puke on a fact-finding mission had decided that this combat-hewn jungle fighter had been a little lax in his selection of targets in proximity to civilian populations. What with the climate of the times toward the end of the war, the Congressman, whose idea of fighting a war must have originated in an Ivy League fencing arena, was able to generate enough heat to bring about a court martial. Despite the Colonel's strong defense of the man in question as a patriot, the legislator, who bordered on being a communist sympathizer, succeeded in his quest and the man was unceremoniously dismissed to civilian life.

Colonel Dubach knew that this former soldier now functioned in the netherworld of mercenaries, that he was still grateful for the Colonel's stance in his defense, and that he would be willing to help the Colonel however he could.

This was how the Colonel came to be driving toward a warehouse off Oriole Beach Road, in an area of Gulf Breeze where tourists never go – or even suspect exists. In his shirt pocket was a crumpled piece of paper, provided by his former subordinate, with an address and the name Dickerson Banner scribbled on it.

Dickerson Banner, known as "Sonny," did not start life as a criminal; a little luck here, a little luck there, and who knows? He could have been a politician. "Modest" was how a person might describe Sonny's formative years. Not trailer-park modest, but frame-house-working-class modest. Sonny's dad was a postal employee; his mom brought in some additional revenue as a teacher's aide when she wasn't having babies. Sonny had three brothers, none of whom were bad kids in the sense of evil or willfully malicious. They just didn't get a lot of supervision.

In generations prior, Sonny and his brothers might have been celebrated by Mark Twain: *Sonny Banner and Huckleberry Finn.* But as things were in the last half of the twentieth century, sanctions tended to come from the government – as in the police – as opposed to the community, in instances where the parents didn't have time to care, or maybe just didn't care.

Perhaps it was because Sonny was the eldest, the test case for his parents, that he turned down the wrong fork in the road once too often. Or maybe it was because he was born on a Wednesday instead of a Friday. For whatever reason, Sonny gravitated to the faster crowd, and ultimately the criminal element. These people became his reference group, and Sonny, a bright fellow, learned well the lessons of the street.

Fairly early on in high school, Sonny

discovered that people wanted many things they could not legally get, and that utilizing his connections, he could meet their needs – for a price. It started with booze. The kids wanted beer for a party. Sonny had older friends who could legally buy it. Sonny brought the buyer and seller together. From booze to drugs to sex, Sonny knew the people, and the more he plied his new trade, the more his capabilities for obtaining forbidden pleasures increased. During his senior year in high school, he realized he was too busy making money to study. So he bought the answers to his final exams, and, while he was at it, he arranged for someone to take his college entrance tests.

College was even better, from Sonny's perspective. He made money hand over fist, and only went to class occasionally to take the tests for which he had purchased the answers. It was during his junior year that some freshman, unhappy with the midterm answers Sonny had sold him, had called foul and went to the administration. Sonny was out of college and indicted for theft.

The resulting brief probated sentence and Sonny's new status as a non-college student weren't all that bad. In his line of work, he could make more money than a college degree would ever have provided. So Sonny applied himself, and in short order entered the fast lane as a full-blown player.

Like professional athletes deluged with sudden wealth at a young age and bereft of experience, Sonny did the inevitable. He got careless. Attempting to procure a call girl for a client, Sonny inadvertently recruited an undercover vice cop. This was a bit more serious than selling exams, and, because of his former offense, despite his age, the honorable court assessed five years in state prison. It was a lot like granting Sonny a scholarship to the criminal graduate school of his choice.

On his release, older, wiser, and hardened, Sonny decided he was way too well known in his hometown. In fact, he decided the state was a bit constricting.

Looking about for a likely location, he chanced upon the Florida Panhandle, specifically Pensacola. In addition to a populace who would now and again want things that were frowned upon by the community, there were gazillions of military types. Healthy young guys who wanted to party hearty when they weren't learning the arts of war which they might be called upon to demonstrate to their detriment at any time.

Besides that, Sonny had chanced upon some former Pensacola natives, currently indisposed by prison bars, who had given Sonny the inside track on how to wheel and deal on the Emerald Coast.

Sonny had lived cautiously, at least as cautiously as a criminal can, and prospered. If you wanted it, and the law said you couldn't have it, Sonny was the man. But you had to have references.

Studying his piece of paper, Ruston Dubach pulled his older model Lincoln into the driveway of Sonny's warehouse and walked to the small entrance beside the garage doors. Although the Colonel was a man of experience, it was not this kind of experience. He wasn't sure whether one knocked first or just walked in. Rethinking the matter and deciding that bursting in on a criminal might result in being shot, he knocked.

"Come," came the response. The Colonel couldn't know that his Lincoln had been monitored on Sonny's surveillance camera from the moment it entered the driveway.

Dubach stepped into the rather massive, dimly lit room, squinting about for his contact. What he saw was an incredible collection of items, from powerboats to framed pictures. This place could have been a flea market. Finally, his gaze settled on a seemingly young man coming toward him through what the Colonel assumed was an office door.

To his surprise, Sonny wasn't big and hairy and covered with tattoos. On the contrary, the approaching man was of medium build, wearing a bright Hawaiian shirt, longish shorts of neutral color, and sandals. It was difficult to tell his hair color, as he sported a baseball cap with the bill backwards.

"What can we do for ya?" queried Sonny.

"Eh, I'm looking for Dickerson Banner," the Colonel answered.

"That would be me, and who might you be?"

"Colonel Ruston Dubach, retired of course, and I was told you'd be expecting me."

Sonny stood quietly, looking the Colonel over. The Colonel began to fidget.

"Yeah, you're about what I expected, but just in case, how 'bout some ID?"

The Colonel chose not to take offense at Sonny's manner, and produced his driver's license. Sonny studied the license, then the Colonel.

"Our mutual friend says you're good people. So how can I help out?" asked Sonny.

Once again, the Colonel wasn't sure of his

ground. Should he speak in hint and innuendo, or come directly to the point? Clearly this man wasn't going to help him state his case. He decided directness had always served him well in the past.

"I need plastic explosives, detonators, and timers sufficient to bring down a substantial structure." He waited.

"I can do that," replied Sonny with a smile, "but it's gonna cost ya."

"We understand that, Mr. Banner," was the Colonel's immediate response.

"Sonny. Call me Sonny. May I ask exactly what you intend to blow up?"

"You may ask, but I'd prefer that to be my sole concern. My ... our mutual friend didn't say you'd need that information." The Colonel was beginning to have second thoughts.

Sonny raised both hands in a gesture of placation. "Not a problem. I got the goods. You got the money. We do the deal. Arm's length. No sweat."

Sonny ushered the Colonel into his office, which, to the Colonel's surprise, was quite well-furnished; there they worked out the details of the quantity, the price, and the logistics of the swap in a businesslike fashion. Concluding the negotiations, the Colonel stood to leave. Neither man offered his hand.

Watching his TV monitor as the Colonel drove out of the parking area, Sonny mulled the situation over. What the man wanted was no problem, but there might be a secondary play here. He would know soon enough what this man intended to blow up, and thereafter it might be worth a little extra cash for his silence. Tricky, without taking the fall with him, but maybe there was a way.

Or perhaps a little tip to the right person ahead of time might translate into some brownie points with the local law enforcement. A man in this business can't have too many favors owed by the police.

Sonny smiled to himself.

CHAPTER 11

A person unfamiliar with island ways might have thought that the University of Florida was on the Florida State ten-yard line, late in the fourth quarter, with the score tied ten-to-ten. Wandering into Bobby D's, that person would have found the Wooliebooger Militia gripping cold beers and staring intently at the TV. Venturing down beach, he would have discovered Charlie and Lula were likewise transfixed at Peg Leg's upstairs bar. Across Santa Rosa Sound, in America, an eerie silence surrounded the sheriff and his wife as they eyed the tube in McGuire's Irish Pub, a most peculiar place to experience quiet. Even Sonny Banner stared, over a hamburger and fries that sat on his desk, at the television mounted high on his office wall.

The object of their attention was not, in fact, a sporting event, but the Weather Channel.

*****

Jordan Faith was sitting across a bar-like desk from James Singer, who was serving up softballs for Faith to knock out of the park.

"Jordan, could you tell us a little about the characteristics of this hurricane?" Singer looked intently interested in whatever wisdom might issue from the older man.

"James, we've seen Jorge move rapidly up the Saffir-Simpson Scale from disorganized convection to a mammoth hurricane. Frankly, I'm not sure I can remember a hurricane developing this fast and this powerfully."

The camera focused on Singer's face, clearly displaying the thought that if Jordan Faith didn't remember it, it hadn't happened.

"We have word now," the older man advised, "from the hurricane hunters that Hurricane Jorge has sustained winds of one hundred and fifteen miles an hour and gusts to one hundred and thirty."

"Wow!" exclaimed Singer. "That would be a Category Three on the Saffir-Simpson, wouldn't it, Jordan?"

"That's right, James. And it looks like it's gaining strength toward a Category Four." Jordan Faith nodded gravely.

"Tell our viewers what Category Three

means, Jordan."

"Well, James, that means that Jorge carries a storm surge of from nine to twelve feet, depending on the tidal flow, and is capable of doing extensive damage to coastal areas." Jordan frowned, his eyes reflecting that he'd seen it all before and this was bad.

"Gee, Jordan, should evacuation procedures be initiated?" James Singer looked like he might be ready to run out of the studio if Jordan said it was time.

"No, James." Jordan kind of snickered, and eyed the camera like he was a little embarrassed for this naive alarmist. "It's a bit premature for that."

The picture shifted to what looked like a giant coconut donut with frayed edges.

"You can see here," Jordan continued, as he drew a yellow squiggle which appeared over the hole in the donut, "that's the eye of the hurricane. We have it at 55° west longitude and still 23.5° north latitude, headed due west at, now, thirty miles an hour.

"Now over here, you don't see much 'cause there's not much to see." Jordan drew a yellow line to the east. "But over here are the Bahamas and Miami, and down here Puerto Rico, the Dominican Republic, Haiti, and Cuba." Again he drew a yellow line and swirled it around each potential destination as he said the name.

Looking at Jordan's squiggles, the viewing audience could see that the giant storm was headed dead bang for the Bahamas and Miami, and that the Leeward Islands had better button up for tropical storm conditions, or even hurricane conditions, just in case Jorge jogged south.

"Do you think Jorge will continue on its current path?" asked Singer with great sincerity.

"Well, as you know, James, hurricanes are unpredictable things. But, so far, Jorge has stuck on the Tropic of Cancer like glue." Jordan raised his head and thoughtfully stroked the loose skin under his chin.

"So, Jordan, if you were guessing – and, of course, here at the Weather Channel we don't do that – would you say this bad boy is making a bee line for the Bahamas, Cuba, and the Keys?"

Jordan nodded soberly, and the camera faded to a commercial.

*****

Of course, everybody in Florida is always concerned about an approaching hurricane, regardless of the exact point of landfall. But in this case, the viewing audience around Pensacola was making a mental projection of Jorge's path after Cuba and the Keys. It looked like bull's-eye should be Brownsville, Texas. But for several years now, instead of following the linear projected path, hurricanes entering the Gulf of Mexico had turned north. And north, against all odds, had repeatedly meant Mobile, Pensacola, Panama City, and other places in the Florida Panhandle. In the bars and TV rooms in the area, there was an instant of thoughtful silence before the normal crowd noise resumed.

Slidell and Daphne had finished their dinner and a couple of microbrews at McGuire's, and were now headed home – Daphne driving.

"So, honey," Daphne led off, in a kind of sexy singsong, rubbing Slidell's leg after shifting into fourth gear, "What's new with the Charlie Cross thing?"

Slidell hated this part of being married to someone in criminal defense. Theoretically, law enforcement, as the name says, just objectively enforces the laws, but that wasn't quite all of it. A person couldn't put in long hard hours trying to accomplish a goal without becoming emotionally involved. When an officer worked to put together a case, and chased down a bad guy who might reasonably be expected to put up some kind of fight, he wanted that bad guy to stay chased down. He didn't want the guy back out on the street, where he would probably continue being a bad guy, hurt some innocent citizen, and create the need to be chased down again.

On the other side, Slidell knew the Constitution guaranteed those accused of a crime the right to have an attorney. He knew that didn't mean the accused got to have someone who had just passed the bar sit beside him and do nothing. It meant that the duty, not the job, of that defense attorney was to walk that bad guy – guilty, innocent, or unknown – right out of the jail, or as close to that as possible. As often as not, that meant convincing a judge or jury or both that the arresting officer was at best an incompetent fool and at worst a malicious rogue, far worse than the criminals with which he dealt.

Slidell found it easy to see how there might be a little friction between law enforcement and criminal defense. A police officer can have his whole week brightened by the mere act of writing a traffic ticket to a member of the defense bar, whereas it was always pleasant for the defense side to read about a cop being busted for misconduct.

The two sides are natural enemies.

However, despite the general hostility, he knew there would always be instances, not unlike the Montagues and the Capulets, when a cop would couple with a defense lawyer. Clearly, this was the situation in which they found themselves. Slidell recognized that he was in bed with the defense, literally. So, if by some weird happenstance, Daphne Fairhope seemed to know a little bit more about the state's case than she was supposed to, it looked real bad for Slidell.

But both Slidell and Daphne felt that if anybody in their right mind thought two people in the same field could avoid talking shop, they'd somehow confused this place with a perfect world. So they had settled on the inevitable next best thing – we can talk, but neither of us can use insider information. Kind of like the priest and the penitent. Nevertheless, it was still hard. Although neither Daphne nor Slidell liked sharing information, the dislike was more than offset by the mutual interest such conversations created and the feeling of being privy to something other people would never know.

"Don't think that dog'll hunt," Slidell finally answered Daphne's question. He found that saying something colloquial was a lot easier somehow than the blunt truth in precise English.

Daphne pondered Slidell's statement briefly, then guessed, "Could that mean forensics disagreed with your deputy's assessment of the substance in question?"

Slidell frowned and smacked his lips. "It's a possibility. But, then, anything is possible," he teased, using the classic police dodge to cross-examination from the defense during trial.

"Well, Sheriff, let me ask you this," she got in the spirit of the game of cross-examination. "You would agree that in the case of a person arrested for felony possession of cocaine, the normal procedure would be to present the case to the grand jury?"

"Grunt," said Slidell.

"I'm sorry, Sheriff. Our court reporter can't record a grunt. You'll have to answer yes or no," chided Daphne. "Assuming, then, that the normal procedure wasn't followed, why do you, as the High Sheriff of Escambia County, believe this would be?"

"Because the dumb ass deputy relied on an anonymous tip to begin with. And the same said dumb ass then failed to field test the substance he discovered," growled Slidell, breaking character.

Slidell was teasing, but he was not happy about what had happened. The bantering atmosphere evaporated. Both people knew that an anonymous tip was not near strong enough to allow the search of what, in this case, was a person's residence.

Deputy Atwood had shattered the law, and Slidell wondered why on earth an experienced deputy would do that. Perhaps Atwood had anticipated that Cross would be home, and he would merely ask him if he could search the boat. Slidell was always amazed at the number of people who would give permission to an officer to search just on the basis of a simple request, even when they knew their illegal drugs were on the premises. Maybe, when Atwood didn't find Cross at home, he thought he would have a look-see. If there was no dope, that would be that. If there was, he could come back. Then Cross arrived right in the middle of the search, and he had to do something. Life can be a slippery slope, Slidell philosophized.

Daphne was thinking that she wished she and her husband didn't have a deal. She had a hearing on this issue very shortly, and she already knew what was going to happen. Besides, this little situation had the feel of a federal civil rights lawsuit. Now she had a problem, aside from making everyone needlessly go through the motions of a hearing that could be avoided. She represented Charlie Cross, but she couldn't use what she had just learned for Charlie's benefit. She figured that using this kind of information had to be part of what the Attorney's Canon of Ethics called "zealous representation," something she was bound to do for her clients, even if it was actually William Norton's oath and not her own yet.

This was shaping up to be a terrific game of "pretend," like when she was a little girl. She'd just have to pretend she didn't know what she knew, and follow the usual steps. Either that or breach the trust she and Slidell had established. Maybe this was why being in bed with the other side always had negative implications; the odds of a serious conflict of interest were just too great.

CHAPTER 12

Sonny Banner had made the appropriate arrangements, and was now awaiting the delivery of the explosives. He would then make the transfer to Dubach. But Sonny was not an idle or lazy person; he was not content to do business as usual. In his little black heart, he sensed that the explosives deal could be big, and if a person paid attention, big things could spin off big bucks.

The issue had been, what was Dubach going to blow up? At least in theory, it could have been anything. But as a practical matter, Dubach was an old retired military type, and whatever he was going to blow up probably affected him directly. If Dubach had shown up at the warehouse all wild-eyed, spouting radical doctrine, and calling him "brother," his target could have been anything. But Dubach struck Sonny as too old and too tired to do anything but react to something that was upsetting his golden years. At least, that was the way Sonny had it figured.

Given that premise, the situation became manageable. He merely had to make inquiries of some of his contacts among the beach locals who would know, or make it their business to know, if they didn't already. Lots of people owed Sonny favors.

It had only taken a weekend before Sonny knew all there was to know about Colonel Ruston Dubach, Retired, and his existence on the beach. He hung out at Bobby D's, fished, played poker on Wednesday night, and was actively, radically, vocally against the development of the Sandcastle Hotel and Condominiums. Bingo!

At first it was difficult for Sonny to believe that this old dude was a terrorist, but the more he thought about it, the more it seemed, in a way, like a reasonable reaction.

Here was this nice little island where the guy lived, and he liked it just the way it was. Along comes Megabucks Corporation, which managed somehow to convince the local government that it would be a wonderful thing to turn this neat little island into Miami Beach. What's he gonna do? Roll over? No. He's a good American – he knew the democratic process wouldn't let him down. But it did. Too many dollars dancing in too many eyes overriding the pure hearts of the elected officials.

Sonny did not make Colonel Ruston Dubach, Retired, for a crazed maniac killer. In fact, killing was probably the farthest thing from his mind. Sonny's guess was that what Dubach was up to was to create just enough downside to scare off the number crunchers. If they can't build it profitably, they won't come, he mentally paraphrased the line from *Field of Dreams*.

Sonny kind of admired the old man, but thought that the Colonel's problem was that he was too emotionally involved. A more objective person, say himself, might see this as an opportunity. Why not include himself as sort of a silent partner?

Why not, without telling the Wooliebоogers, contact Island Quest, Inc., and threaten to blow up the building if they didn't give him, say, one hundred thousand dollars? If they did, he didn't care if the old man blew up the building or not.

But first he would have to demonstrate that the threat was not to be taken lightly. He would be more adept at this than the Wooliebоogers.

For the inquiring mind, it was refreshing to know that information about almost anything could be accessed through the library. Sonny wasn't really conversant with the Internet, but he did have a passing acquaintance with business finance in college, before they threw him out. It was easy enough to find out a great deal about any publicly traded corporation by looking in *Standard & Poor's*. IQ was publicly traded.

Sonny easily determined that Island Quest, Inc., was incorporated under Delaware law, but their corporate headquarters was home-based in Pensacola. The corporation's major holding was an area of land on Santa Rosa Island, and the corporate officers were listed as Jackson Bolton, President and Chief Executive Officer; Coleman Dunlee, Vice President; and Ada Bolton, Secretary-Treasurer.

Sonny figured Jackson Bolton was "the man," Ada was his wife just holding a place on paper, and Dunlee was a gofer, flunky type who worked for the Boltons. This turned out to be pretty much right on. Therefore, Dunlee was the target.

Sonny had learned from his various mentors and associates in the world of crime that in order to get a victim's attention, his serious attention, it was first necessary to do something serious. In a one-on-one hijack scenario, a good first move was to hit the mark with the gun, or cut him, if you were using a knife. This would usually scare the shit out of him, and, thereafter, he knew you weren't playing around. Of course, bigger stakes demanded more drastic measures.

It had been a simple matter to determine that Coleman Dunlee lived on Ariola Drive on Pensacola Beach – probably, Sonny guessed, in one of the expensive new constructions.

It had also not been difficult for Sonny to case Coleman Dunlee. Coleman had been under the aegis of Jackson Bolton for so long, he feared no evil. Besides that, Coleman must have reasoned, why would anyone want to mess with the flunky? Coleman Dunlee's job was basically to follow Jackson Bolton around and do whatever he was asked to do. Usually, he left his house around seven in the morning, and returned home around seven in the evening. On weekends, he was on call, but he could be predictably found at the oldest beach bar on the island – The Islander.

No one had paid much attention to the man strolling down the beach; nor had anyone noticed when Sonny casually walked off the beach to the back of Dunlee's house. Smashing a window and entering the house would have been a simple matter, but it wasn't necessary. Dunlee had left the sliding glass door at the rear of the house unlocked. All Sonny had to do was wait for the lord of the manor to return home.

Like clockwork, as the ultra-modern glass wall clock struck seven, Sonny heard the key in the door. Again second guessing, Sonny had figured Dunlee's first move on returning home after work would be to get a beer out of the refrigerator.

He had been right, and when Coleman Dunlee popped the top, Sonny popped the cap.

The man never knew what hit him. Sonny watched him crumple to the floor, then twitch briefly as his life and the beer ran out on the floor.

It had not been necessary for Sonny to terrorize the man before he killed him. All he needed was Dunlee dead, and something distinctive at the scene that the police would communicate to Jackson Bolton. When he made his demands, he would note this thing, and Bolton would know.

Sonny leaned down and dipped his finger in the dead man's blood. On the refrigerator he wrote "Bye Bye Bolton."

*****

A short time later, Jackson Bolton sat at his desk, working late, reviewing the costs to date at the Sandcastle worksite.

He was interrupted by his secretary's matter-of-fact announcement over the office intercom. "Mr. Bolton, there's a Mr. Brown on the phone for you." Encountering silence at the other end, she continued, "Mr. Brown says he's calling from the Sandcastle site, and needs to speak with you urgently."

What now? Bolton thought. Engaging the appropriate line, he answered "Bolton."

"Mr. Bolton, I have a business proposition for you," said the voice on the other end of the line.

Bolton waited, fearing that some salesman had just sidestepped his secretary.

"You give me one hundred thousand dollars, and I won't blow up the Sandcastle Hotel."

This definitely got Jackson Bolton's attention. "Who is this?" he spluttered into the phone. "Is this some kind of a joke?"

"No joke. Just listen," intoned the dead voice. "I'll contact you with the details in a few days. You just get the money together. Pay the money, and I go away ... forever. Do not contact the police. Think of it as a business expense. Bye. Bye. Bolton." Sonny let the last three clearly enunciated words hang in the air.

The line went dead.

CHAPTER 13

Earlier on the same day that Sonny Banner was effecting Coleman Dunlee's demise, Charlie Cross was walking down the corridor of M. C. Blanchard Judicial Building in downtown Pensacola. He was too preoccupied with his own problems to notice the other people crowding the hall, also waiting for their time in court.

Mostly they looked like Charlie did on any given day but this one. These were not sophisticated people, by and large. They were people who, by reason of their upbringing, or lack of it, had problems maintaining their lives within the boundaries proscribed by law and society. Most wore the clothes they wore every other day of their life, whether that meant shorts and a t-shirt or something more formal, like jeans and a t-shirt. Few had seen the need to acquire a white shirt and tie, not to mention a suit or sport coat, just as they hadn't seen the need not to do dope, take things that didn't belong to them, or punch out the dude who slighted them in a bar. It was how they dealt with life, for better or worse.

Now and again there would be a person dressed like Charlie. Someone who had, by hook or crook, acquired the clothes their lawyer said they should wear to court. To the rest, such a thing was truly beyond their means or just too much trouble or both. Unfortunately, for those who elected to do like they always did, their dress would be one of the first judgment criteria used to determine their future designation as "criminal" or "not-criminal."

Charlie wasn't thinking about that, though. He had instinctively and by training known what a person wears to court. What Charlie was concerned about was locating the 409th Criminal Circuit Court and his one-and-a-half lawyers.

In his heart of hearts, Charlie knew he was not guilty of anything. Just as surely as he knew he was guiltless, he knew his odds of going to prison were high. A judge or jury didn't know Charlie was innocent; they just had his word. The word of a beach bum, who might be able to garner ten other beach bums to come to court and say Charlie had a good reputation for truth and veracity. Big deal.

On the other side of the coin, there would be the police officer who, even if it was Atwood the fat and horrible, would seem to have no reason to lie, and who would appear in court in uniform as one of the gallant few standing between good citizens and predatory criminals at the risk of his own life.

Besides that, this wasn't a case of he-said-she-said. This was a drug offense. Charlie knew his own government had declared war on drugs, drug users, and drug dealers, and now the accusing finger of guilt had pointed to the object of just indignation – Charlie Cross. The prosecutor would do likewise, pointing his finger at Charlie Cross while challenging the judge or jury to do the right thing, save our homes and our children, put this affront to decency away forever. And they would listen, and they would do it. Or so Charlie's thoughts ran.

Finally, Charlie stood at the big double doorway marked "409th Criminal Circuit Court of Escambia County." It might as well have read "Abandon Faith All Ye Who Enter Here." Charlie did not see the silver lining, and he didn't see his lawyer-and-a-half, either.

William Norton, unlike Charlie Cross, did not work particularly hard in any school – high school or college – and he was extremely lucky to get into law school at all. But William Norton was smart, too smart by half some said, and that meant he had an outstanding score on the Law School Aptitude Test, which tended to measure innate ability. Reference letters from a couple of alumni who had contributed greatly to the law school clinched his acceptance. William's father was a solid member of the good ol' rich boys club.

In law school, William continued to be the champion of the "gentleman's C," and graduated somewhere near the bottom of his class. Most of his classmates and law professors were frankly shocked when William logged the highest bar exam score of the year and the second highest in the history of the state. William Norton was a natural, and he was attracted to the practice of criminal law.

Like most pursuits in life, when school is finally out, the real learning, the practical side of education, begins. One of the best graduate schools in criminal law is the local prosecutor's office. The drill after that is learning by doing, and if a person sticks with it long enough, he can become quite proficient. This was the route William Norton chose.

From the beginning, "Wild Bill," as the office christened him, showed great promise as a trial prosecutor. Although he wasn't crazy about learning the law, he loved the aspect of showmanship that was demanded of a successful trial lawyer, and developed something of a cult following for his courtroom antics. The collegial milieu of the office only added to Norton's love for his work.

Moreover, Norton had found that the prosecutor's office consisted mostly of highly intelligent and aggressive twenty-somethings, who had just been released from three-plus years of competitive academic confinement. Even those who had sought to merely graduate from law school had found it necessary to put normal young adult urges on hold. At the prosecutor's office, they found themselves with lots more time and with lots of similarly situated members of the opposite sex, all learning through the trial-by-fire method together. A boot-camp-like bonding took place, not bound by many social mores. The moniker, Wild Bill, was not simply the result of William's courtroom behavior. Wild Bill was an animal in trial and on the party scene.

After five years of learning many things about criminal law and life, William set aside the "Wild," and moved to the dark side, as prosecutors chose to characterize criminal defense work. One of the ideas that William had absorbed in the courthouse was that if he stayed too long with the office, he would never leave. He would become institutionalized, so to speak. A government hack.

In fairly short order, William Norton became a successful criminal defense lawyer. With the courtroom skills he had developed in the prosecutor's office, and more than his share of natural talent, he had an uncanny ability to establish reasonable doubt in the minds of jurors. William Norton was also quite chummy with the judiciary. Along the way, he had even developed an expertise in law, which he now worked to maintain.

No longer needing to fit in with a group of underpaid peers, his personal style had changed radically to expensive clothes and even more expensive cars. To see William Norton was to know he was a thoroughbred. It would cost you, but he'd take you to the roses.

Charlie didn't have a watch and hadn't had one in some time. So he just paced and fretted. Now we're gonna be late, and someone's gonna be pissed.

"Hey, chill, dude," came a voice from his left. "Man, you're givin' me the heebie-jeebies just watchin' you. Your lawyer'll get here when he gets here." This from a skinny old dude who looked like he lived under a pier on the beach.

Charlie was about to ask him how he knew he was waiting for his lawyer, when he felt a hand touch his sleeve.

"Mr. Cross! Sorry we're late. Mr. Norton got hung up in a hearing down the hall." It was Daphne Fairhope, looking every bit as good as the first time Charlie met her, albeit a bit more lawyerly in a navy blue suit.

"Oh, it's OK," replied Charlie, and he actually meant it. "Just a little nervous, I guess. I've never done this before."

Now things seemed to be back on track, and something in Daphne's manner was very comforting – like she actually cared, with something almost like pain in her eyes for Charlie's predicament.

"There's nothing to worry about, Mr. Cross. Today's just a motion hearing. Mr. Norton thinks the material seized might have been acquired illegally. If that's true, it can't be introduced into evidence, and the state's case goes up in smoke." Daphne tilted her head slightly, questioning if Charlie understood.

Charlie nodded that he did.

"Regardless of what happens today," Daphne continued, "this will force the state to produce the alleged controlled substance, and we will request that we be allowed to have our chemist analyze a sample. We still don't know how much they seized, or even what it really was." Daphne mentally grimaced. "It was only cocaine in the cop's opinion, and the state has been stonewalling our requests for discovery. In any case, you won't go to jail today. It's not a hearing for an assessment of guilt."

Charlie knew that, but he was relieved to hear it from his lawyer, or half-a-lawyer, as the case may be.

As Charlie was letting all that Daphne was saying sink in, his concentration was interrupted by the arrival of a neatly coiffured man in a very nice suit wearing a diamond pinky ring and some sort of large gold watch.

"Mr. Norton, this is Charlie." Daphne made the introductions. Charlie immediately recognized that he had been demoted from "Mr. Cross," and was the number two name in the introduction.

William Norton extended his hand, much like he was allowing Charlie to kiss his pinky ring, and gave a perfunctory smile.

"Nice to meet you, Charlie," he clipped. "Are we ready?"

"Yes, sir," Daphne responded briskly.

Charlie nodded, and off they went through the big double doors. Looking back as they moved toward the courtroom, Charlie saw the skinny dude roll his eyes and purse his lips, as if to say "Whoa, you got the big dog."

Norton motioned for Charlie to sit in the gallery, and signaled for Daphne to follow him. As they passed the invisible line beyond which laymen do not pass in a courtroom, the judge looked up from whatever he was doing on the bench.

"Well, Mr. Norton. Always a pleasure to have you in our court. What brings you here today?"

From a judge, that was encouraging, mused Charlie.

Norton apparently introduced Daphne to the judge, after which there was a round of chuckling. Charlie could only make out something about "sheriff," and figured they all thought it was funny that the sheriff's wife was representing a criminal. Then they huddled.

At that moment, Charlie felt much like a bug under a microscope. Humiliated. Vulnerable. Subject to forces over which he had no control. This was worse than the arrest. He knew the others in the gallery – witnesses, other defendants, interested spectators – were watching the show, looking at Charlie with the single question: wonder what he did?

Up at the bench, Charlie saw Norton step back and look dubiously at the judge.

"They did what?" Norton's voice boomed.

Charlie thought he saw the judge flinch before he shrugged and said something Charlie couldn't hear.

Making an impatient gesture of departure, Norton turned on his heel and was out of the courtroom before Charlie could say "what's going on?" Daphne Fairhope followed, gesturing for Charlie to step out into the hall.

In the hall, there was no evidence that William Norton had ever been there. Somewhere in his imagination, Charlie thought there would at least be a trail of sparks.

"You're free to go, Mr. Cross. Your case has been dismissed," said Daphne with a smile.

Charlie looked puzzled.

"Whatever it was that Atwood took off of your boat, it wasn't cocaine. The prosecutors finally got around to sending it to forensics, and the forensics boys said not dope. So that's pretty much it. There might be some sort of civil rights action you can take, but I really can't advise you in that area. I can recommend a civil attorney, if you want to look into it."

Charlie allowed as how he'd think about it, thanked Daphne, and wandered off toward his car. Daphne scurried off in the direction that Charlie supposed William Norton had gone. As he passed the skinny dude, the dude gave him a crooked smile and a big winking nod.

Charlie knew he should have felt relieved, but that wasn't exactly what he felt. It was like he had just had sex but didn't even get a handshake afterwards.

CHAPTER 14

Charlie Cross lay on his side, supporting his head with his left hand. He wasn't trying to even out his tan, or deal with skull cramps brought on by too much drinking the evening prior. If he maintained this position, he could take in the panorama of the aqua gulf lapping on the sugar-white sand and gradually changing to deep blue as the unseen sea bed sloped away from the land. Of course, a person could do this without lifting his head at such an angle, but then he couldn't have seen over, and included in his view, the sun-browned, marvelously shaped body of Tallulah Vidalia, who was lying beside him on her back.

Several hours before, Charlie had awakened to a glorious day and decided to knock off from his hectic schedule of lurking around waiting for someone to hire him to do something. As it turned out, Lula's dance card also had an open space, so they packed a picnic lunch, iced down some beer, and took the *Long Gone* down Santa Rosa Sound just beyond Pensacola Pass.

If a person continued west on the Intracoastal Waterway from the pass, and hung a really hard left at the first opportunity, there was a secluded bay with a white sand beach – a perfect anchorage. And if one crossed that spit of sand, which had been the location of Fort McRee prior to the Civil War and currently formed the tip of the barrier island of Perdido Key, to the gulf side, the isolation was complete.

Now, with the sun pleasantly baking in its warmth, Charlie was absent-mindedly dividing his attention between the Gulf and the muscle tone of Lula's cocoa-colored stomach where it was interrupted by the neon yellow of her bikini bottom. As he began to feel a stirring somewhere in his groin, his attention inexplicably turned to his recent legal problems. That kind of interruption wouldn't have happened a few years ago – he briefly wondered about the merits of Viagra – but now his mental track had changed.

"Lula, did I ever thank you for calling that lawyer the other night?" he queried.

"Mmmm," purred Lula

"Well, if I didn't, I sure do. A jail is no place for an innocent man." Charlie's mind flashed back to the jail tank. He shook his head to clear the memory.

"I guess she's pretty good. She called me yesterday after the hearing, and wanted to know if I wanted to pursue the civil rights matter. When I asked what that meant, she said maybe we could set up some kind of a hearing, maybe subpoena the sheriff's records. Find out what the deal was. I said I'd think about it, and let her know. What do you think?"

"Oh, I don't know, Charlie," Lula stretched and rolled over on her stomach. "Let sleepin' dogs lie?"

Charlie was momentarily distracted by Lula's shape. She moved like a cat.

"You know, if I ever thought I'd go back into law," Charlie wondered aloud, "I'd see if we could get the arrest record expunged, if they do that here. But, as it stands, it's probably not worth the time and money." He realized he was talking to himself. "Who do you suppose would have put that stuff on my boat and then tipped the cops?"

Charlie noticed that Lula was undoing her top, to avoid a tan line, he supposed. But tan line or no, he was now lying next to a mostly naked woman on a very deserted beach – he ran his index finger salaciously down Lula's back.

"Do you suppose anyone is likely to be

comin' by any time soon?" she breathed, as she slid her left hand down Charlie's chest into his bathing suit.

Charlie sure didn't care.

*****

Over the pass, through the National Seashore, and about ten miles east, sexual foreplay was not the order of the day. There was no tanned curvaceous body to form the base of Slidell Goodbee's visual picture of the gulf; only a credenza. There he sat, feet up, pondering the meaning of the sudden outbreak of mysterious deaths.

It had been a couple of years since there had been a violent death on the island, not counting jet skis running into each other or over swimmers. Now all of a sudden he had two. One was clearly a murder, carried out execution style; the other was a maybe. Other than the fact that the two bodies had been discovered in the same general location on the island and that the two dead guys both worked for Island Quest, Inc., the deaths didn't seem to be related.

So, for the time being, he would set poor old Hulen Puckett aside and try to focus on Coleman

Dunlee. The question was, why would anyone want to kill Dunlee?

Slidell had been aware of Dunlee for about as long as he could remember, and there was nothing distinguishing about the man at all. He had grown up in Pensacola, and, for as long as Slidell knew, had been a flunky for Jackson Bolton, even in high school. Apparently, Bolton paid Dunlee pretty well, which enabled him to move to one of the island's nicer locations several years ago. Slidell supposed that some people were jealous, but that kind of jealousy didn't usually provoke murder. Dunlee had been arrested for driving under the influence awhile back, but otherwise, he had no criminal record. The man had never been married, so there was no ex-wife, jealous wife, or any kind of wife out there with a motive to kill. If Coleman Dunlee was going to be murdered for any reason, Slidell figured it would have been some kind of spontaneous killing in anger, but that wasn't the way this one came down. Blank. Blank. And blank.

In Slidell's experience, when people were killed execution-style, there was usually a "professional" involved. That suggested a money motive. Although Dunlee wasn't reputed to be a gambler, some sort of unpaid debt to a bookie, or some such person, might have gotten him killed. He'd have one of his deputies check that out.

The other, more obvious, motive that presented itself to Slidell was something related to his job. Maybe an act of disloyalty being avenged, or, as a named officer in IQ, perhaps he had suffered for the corporation's misdeeds. This angle was, of course, underscored by the strange inscription on Dunlee's refrigerator, and that fact bothered Slidell. Why would a professional killer leave a clue?

With those things in mind, Sheriff Goodbee made two calls. The first was to his chief deputy, directing him to begin investigating Dunlee's proclivity for gaming. The second was to Jackson Bolton.

Jackson Bolton had been sitting in his office wondering where Coleman Dunlee was and why he wasn't where he was supposed to be, which was here waiting for Jackson to tell him what to do. This wouldn't have normally been so irritating, but Jackson had had a dream the night before about finding a large fish wrapped in newspaper, and he woke up hungry. He had interpreted his nocturnal fantasy to mean that some cosmic force was advising him to grill fish for dinner, perhaps amberjack. Now he wanted Coleman to run down to Joe Patti's Seafood Company and buy the fixings.

Usually aggressive, not normally phone-shy, he had flinched when the telephone on his desk rang. That crazy call he'd received last night had apparently had an effect.

"What? Who is it? Coleman?" he demanded into the receiver.

"Coleman's still not here, Mr. Bolton. It's Sheriff Goodbee on line two," advised his secretary.

He punched the button activating line two. "Sheriff," his voice became animated and friendly, "what can I do for you?"

"Mr. Bolton, I've got bad news for you. Coleman Dunlee's been killed." Silence at the other end.

Slidell hated delivering this kind of news to friends and loved ones. He even hated the words of announcement. Wasn't there a better way to deliver such news? Sugarcoat it? Ease into it? But he had determined that there was just no other way: get it out and get it over with. Slidell figured it wouldn't make any difference if you handed the bereaved a check for a million dollars along with the news that their child had been found dead. Nothing could lessen that pain.

But now there were other factors at work. Jackson Bolton's reaction to the news might go a long way in explaining why Coleman Dunlee had to die.

"Are you sure, Sheriff? Could there have been some mistake?"

"No, Mr. Bolton. Sorry. There's no question."

There was another pause, then, "You said 'killed.' Was it some kind of accident or something?"

"Mr. Bolton, it seems Coleman Dunlee was murdered." How else could he say it?

"Nooo. Why would anyone want to murder Coleman? Everyone liked him." Bolton's voice keened.

Slidell allowed time for Bolton to compose himself, then continued. "We don't know, Mr. Bolton, but I'd like to ask you some questions, if you're up to it."

Slidell went through the usual kinds of questions, looking for possible motives, but Bolton knew nothing helpful. As Slidell brought the interview to a close, he popped the big one.

"Do the words 'Bye Bye Bolton' mean anything to you beyond the obvious?"

Now there was a peculiar silence. Bolton had

covered the receiver. If Slidell could have heard what was happening on the other end, the sound would have been an unmistakable gag. When the background noise returned, Bolton's voice was composed.

"No. I can't think of any special meaning that would have. You know? I mean, beyond the obvious. Why? Should it mean something special to me?"

"Those words were found at the crime scene. I was hoping they would mean something to you, but if they don't ... " Slidell let his voice trail off.

Slidell didn't mention the exact circumstances of the discovery. He didn't want to cause Bolton more pain than necessary. Also, he needed to withhold some information just in case he got a confession. He'd be able to verify the killer's version of the crime with facts no one else could know.

The sheriff thanked Bolton for his cooperation, advised that he might be back in touch to clear up some other matters if they arose, and rang off.

Thinking through the conversation, several things seemed clear to Slidell. Bolton had not known of the death. His general reaction was just what one would expect from a friend under these circumstances. But his reaction to the last question could signify that Bolton was holding something back. Or, maybe he was just having a delayed reaction to the unexpected news. Whatever, Slidell shrugged, it would still be premature to cross Bolton off his mental list of "might-bes."

Jackson Bolton sat in silence. The shock of the sheriff's last question had caused him to become physically ill. His mind could not readily conceive that the death of his friend was somehow related to the crazy extortion call. But, on another level, he knew it had to be. Someone had killed his friend to make a point.

CHAPTER 15

John Thomas Taylor sat in the top of the old kerosene-powered lighthouse on the island of San Salvador (74.30° west longitude; 24.05° north latitude). The island, formerly called Watling, was believed to be the first step-off point for Christopher Columbus in the new world. John Taylor was not thinking about Christopher Columbus, but instead was thinking himself a truly ignorant man.

John Taylor was a good man, a hard working man, a married man with five children; he mentally checked off his better points. John Taylor was charged with the responsibility of winding the lighthouse machinery four times a day so the light would revolve and alert any ships approaching the Bahamian shores of the danger of running aground. Why, though, had he not heeded the radio bulletins warning of the approaching hurricane?

John Taylor had lived his entire life on the

tiny island of San Salvador and experienced many hurricane warnings. How many times had he been told "you and your family must evacuate?" How many times had he watched as the great storms went north or south, only causing a cloudy day for his island? And when they did hit his island, lawn chairs at the hotels and coconuts were the only casualties. That was why he had decided to ride out the storm. It had been a good decision, he told himself.

Now he watched as mammoth swells crashed over the sandy beach, forcing their briny fingers through the collapsing beach dwellings. The demon winds roared like a hundred jet airplanes, like the ones that normally ferried the rich tourists to the island. As soon as he wound the wheels one last time, he would race for the shelter where his wife and children waited. Perhaps it was even now too late. Tears of fear and sorrow began to stream from John Taylor's eyes. He would miss this life. God save my family, he prayed fervently.

*****

Jordan Faith was standing in the studio of the Weather Channel, waving his outstretched arm and finger at nothing. Dedicated weather watchers who were tuned in on their TVs saw Faith's finger outlining the tip of one of the most easterly islands of the Bahamas.

"About right now, San Salvador is really feeling Jorge's wrath. Our weather satellite has the eye, there," he pointed, "at longitude 73.90° west, latitude 24° north.

"For those of you who have been charting the storm, you'll note it's taken a northward jog. That may be significant, as far as a directional change, or it may be just a wobble. We'll have to wait and see.

"One thing we can tell you is that it's increased in power. The sustained winds are now at one hundred and twenty-five miles an hour, just six miles an hour away from a Category Four. You can see we've extended the warning area from Cuba all the way to up near Jacksonville, Florida. Even if this hurricane moves right through the Florida Straits, where we think it will go, the damage to both Miami and the island of Cuba will be significant.

"But there's still a chance that Jorge will turn north. You see here," he switched maps, "this cold front has moved out of the Rockies. We believe it will move rapidly across Texas, Louisiana, Mississippi, and through Alabama and Florida. If it does what we think it might, it could combine with the gulf stream to move Jorge harmlessly out to-sea.

"It could do that, but, at this point, the computer models predict the front will slow, and Jorge will make landfall in the U.S., probably somewhere around the Keys. This hurricane seems to be maintaining its speed at forty miles an hour for the time being, but probably this group of islands," the map had switched again, and he pointed to the Bahamas chain, "will slow it some. So at this point, we're predicting possible U.S. landfall about this time tomorrow."

Jordan looked worried and tired. "We understand the State of Florida agrees with us. Mandatory evacuation has begun in the Keys, and the city of Miami has been put on full alert status."

The camera switched to a commercial for storm windows and doors.

*****

The Wednesday night poker meeting of the Wooliebooger Militia was in full session, and although they were serious about their card playing, two extraneous topics forced their way into the otherwise standard banter of the poker table.

"Ah do believe you ah bluffin', Colonel," said Chou, as he looked across the dining room table at the four up cards in front of Colonel Dubach. Sure enough they were all red and all hearts, but there was one card still down. Checking the table again, he noted several of the exposed cards were also hearts. "So Ah believe Ah'll jus' call."

The Colonel facially shrugged, as if to say "It's your money."

Tom and Tim were in an intense state of concentration: to fold or not to fold?

Tom, always too easily influenced, flipped his up cards face down in the middle of the table. "I think he's got it. I'm out."

This was no doubt a serious influence on Tim, but he too had observed the number of hearts already distributed. "I'm in. Call your raise."

It seemed neither challenger was confident enough of his determination to raise the stakes of learning the Colonel's hole card. The Colonel smiled, flipping a red ten into the center. The smile was rather sickly, though, as the ten was of diamonds. No flush. No straight. Nothing. "Looks like you boys are too smart for the old Colonel."

Tim grinned widely, turning a two of spades

with a pop as he shifted his eyes to Chou. "That would be two pair, Chou-be-do."

Chou did not like being called Chou-be-do. "Chou" was as close to intimacy as he wanted with Tim, and, besides that, it sounded too much like Scoobedo, the stupid cartoon dog.

"Well, this would be three of a kind, Timmy," mocked Chou, folding over a nine, which matched the other two nines among his up cards.

"Shiiiit!" moaned Tim. "You're the luckiest SOB I ever seen." He emphasized "luckiest," pulling up just short of implying there might be something more to Chou's card playing ability.

The Colonel, sensing the tension, passed the deal and moved to neutral territory. "What's the word on our friend Jorge?"

"Weather guys say that booger is fixin' to smack one of the Keys," responded Tom, eagerly following the Colonel's lead. Tom was not at all comfortable with negative feelings, and this was especially true when they were between his brother and his friend. "If that's the way it falls out, guess where it goes next."

"Nothin' written in stone sayin' it has to visit Pensacola," Chou commented, idly raking in his winnings. "Texas is due a good hurricane. Hell, it might do 'em some good. Theyah always bitchin' about needin' rain."

"I'll tell you what I think." Tim picked up the deal, and was roughly shuffling the cards. "I think Pensacola's gonna get another hurricane, and another, and another 'til they stop being so damned eager to let queers take over our beach every year."

They all knew Tim was referring to the annual Memorial Day Weekend Celebration, when thousands of gays and lesbians congregated on Pensacola Beach. In fact, some folks even referred to the area as the Gay Riviera as a consequence. Tim was mouthing the notion, popularized by the local "Religious Right," that the relatively recent increase in hurricane activity around Pensacola was God's punishment for the city's tolerance of gays.

"Pashaw!" said the Colonel. No one else at the table was old enough to use an expression like that and really mean it.

Tom, never wishing to disagree with the Colonel or his brother, remained silent.

Chou, on the other hand, took this as another opportunity to highlight what he saw as Tim's ignorance. "Why would you think that God loves homosexuals any less than He loves you?" baited Chou. "He made 'em, and if He really doesn't like homosexuals, why'd He do that, do you suppose?"

"The Bible says that homosexuals are an affront to God. That's how I know He don't like 'em. And it just stands to reason that He don't like people who likes people He don't like," Tim argued. "And if that ain't so, how do you explain Pensacola gettin' all these hurricanes, Chou-be-do?"

"Puttin' aside tha issue of whetha oah not you've evah actually read the Bible, Timmy," Chou retorted.

"Tim, would you just deal?" Tom was exasperated.

"I agree with Tom." The Colonel had actually been enjoying the argument, but had noted that Tim didn't seem to be able to deal and argue simultaneously. "Same game?"

Tim sulked momentarily. "No. Not the same game. Some people here are too lucky at five stud. We're gonna play a little draw." Tim began to deal.

"God knows Ah don' wish to change such a fascinatin' topic, but how ah we doin' with owah otha ... situation?" Chou looked at the Colonel.

The Colonel, who had been lightly smiling, turned serious. "Harumph! Gentlemen, I think our ship is about to come in. My, eh, source says he should get the, eh, merchandise tonight. Assuming that to be true, it would be a go for next week."

Tim had stopped dealing again, but the Colonel now was on a topic that took precedence.

"We will follow our usual modus operandi. Since Tim and Tom both have experience with the deployment of this type of merchandise," the Colonel had apparently settled on a pseudonym for explosives, "and are younger, and hence more capable of any necessary climbing, they will handle the placement and timing of the merchandise. Chou and I will be the good eyes, I believe is the expression. Tentatively, next Tuesday sounds right. That will get the job done and put us right back here on our usual Wednesday game with nothing out of the ordinary and no one the wiser."

For once, Tim and Chou were in agreement, *sub silencio*. In fact, all three of them were. The consensus was, Wow! They knew it was coming, but now it was here. Show time.

"Eh, Tim," asked the Colonel, "are you going to deal, or sit there with your mouth open?"

CHAPTER 16

Jackson Bolton was again sitting in the dark in the den of his palatial home perched majestically on the bluffs along Scenic Highway overlooking Escambia Bay. His wife had been curious about such unusual behavior from Jackson earlier in the week. Now she was really getting worried, but she still assumed his actions had something to do with the murder of his longtime friend. Had she known the true reason why Jackson was immobilized in his favorite overstuffed chair, she would have been as troubled as Jackson himself.

Jackson had begun his career in construction with his dad's contracting company. Working initially as unskilled labor on his father's jobsites during summer vacations, he had ample opportunity to learn by watching the various tradesmen practice their craft. Early on, one old electrician was so taken by the speed and facility with which Jackson learned, he rechristened him

Lightnin' – Lightnin' Bolton. And so he was known until he became too rich and important to be called by such a frivolous nickname.

By the time Lightnin' graduated from high school, he had pretty much acquired the skills to be a reasonably good contractor. So, against his dad's wishes, he elected to skip a college education and go into the business. He would liked to have gone into business with his father, but his father had made it abundantly clear that if young Lightnin' didn't go to college, he wasn't going to get any help from home. And that included a job in his father's company.

Most young men might have had second thoughts about jumping out in the cold world alone, but Lightnin' was not only hardheaded, he was also absolutely convinced that college, as far as he was concerned, was a waste of time. The building business was what he wanted to do, and he didn't need a liberal arts education to build a house.

The road to success had been long and difficult: from odd jobs to building spec homes to finally developing subdivisions. He had been grudgingly accepted by the area financial institutions. At first, he had to put up his soul as collateral to get the basic materials with which to build. Now he could walk into any bank in the region and get however much capital he wanted on his signature.

Jackson Bolton had money, but he had earned the money himself and learned hard lessons along the road in so doing. Now some low-life had decided to take some of that money away by force. This caused him much mental anguish.

Jackson knew that one hundred thousand dollars wasn't really much in a development the size of the Sandcastle. He could allot the expense around here and there, jack up the price of this and that, and never even miss it. Presumably, he could then complete his project unmolested, on time, and at the original profit.

However, the idea of rolling over because some dirtball hoodlum, who had no concept of working for what he earned, happened by and wanted to cut himself in, caused the taste of black bile to form in Jackson's throat. Reading of robberies in the news had always infuriated him. Some dildo dufus comes along and says "gimme, cuz I got this gun." It didn't matter how hard the victim had to work for the money, or how much he needed it.

And now it was happening to him. That

didn't even count the killing of his oldest friend just as an opening gambit.

But then, anyone who would do the terrible thing he'd done might do anything. He might kill Jackson's wife next, and still blow up the building. Why not just go with it? It wasn't that big a deal.

Jackson Bolton felt like a tennis ball.

In the end, he reached the only decision with which he could live. He'd sleep on it, but he knew that in the morning he would ring back another old acquaintance: the Escambia County Sheriff.

*****

Sorting through reports by his deputies of things that had gone on in the night, Slidell had been distracted. He knew that Jackson Bolton knew more than he had told, and the sheriff wanted to know what that was. He didn't like having crime in his county, and he especially didn't like having unsolved murders. When his duty officer buzzed in with the news that Jackson Bolton was on the phone, Slidell's mood brightened substantially. Something good was about to happen.

"Goodbee here."

"Sheriff, this is Jackson Bolton, and," he

hesitated, "I didn't tell you the whole truth the last time we talked."

With that predicate, Bolton proceeded to tell the story of the extortion attempt. The sheriff listened attentively, and at the conclusion, they agreed that Bolton would go along with the extortionist's demands, while Slidell set up a trap. There was nothing to do now but wait.

*****

And north of the island, along the side of Bob Sikes Bridge, waiting was what Charlie Cross was doing.

Charlie was standing on the old bridge, now a fishing pier, looking at the calm blue water beneath his rod. Although Charlie wasn't much of a fisherman, once in a while he liked to collect his fishing gear, some bait, and some beer, and try to catch his dinner off the pier.

As he looked around, he noted that some of the folks engaged in the same activity were shirtless. Charlie figured they were either immune to sunburn, or they'd look like lobsters later that night. For himself, he looked much like a Mexican cowboy: long pants, long-sleeved shirt, boots, and a broad-brimmed sombrero. Charlie knew he looked funny, but he knew who would be laughing come nightfall.

He'd been standing in one place for about an hour, and had come to the conclusion that, for some reason, all the little fishes did not like that spot. To his back, he had periodically heard the cries of happy fishermen, but he couldn't see what they were catching because they had set up some kind of tent affair that shielded them from both the sun and their surroundings. Nevertheless, Charlie decided that over there might be a better place to try his luck; he moved to the side of the successful fishermen, but just out of their sight line. He didn't want them to think he was crowding them.

Charlie wasn't really eavesdropping, but he wasn't catching any fish either, so between cars passing on the highway bridge, he was picking up bits and pieces of conversation. At first he wasn't even curious, but after a while, it dawned on him that there was something damned familiar about the voices. He didn't know what, but his focus tightened.

"Where do you suppose the Colonel got the explosives?" Tom was saying, as he raised the line of their string of fish.

"Could have been anywhere, I guess," replied Tim disinterestedly. "I just hope he got enough to blow that piece o' shit high-rise right off its foundations."

Rrrrrrr. Whooosh. Honk. Whoosh. The noise of a group of vehicles apparently launching for the beach from Gulf Breeze caused Charlie to lean toward the tent, almost too far before he caught himself. There was another break.

"Just hope we're ready," noted Tom.

"Hell, Tom, now's as good a time as any, and Tuesday'll be just fine," replied Tim, sounding a note of bravado.

The traffic roared and buzzed and whizzed and generally shut out all other sounds as the evening traffic rush began in earnest. Charlie suddenly realized exactly where he'd heard the voices before and understood the import of what he'd just overheard – they're going to blow up what there was of the new Sandcastle Hotel, and they're going to do it Tuesday.

Still marveling at his discovery, Charlie sensed a movement to his left. He quickly took several steps away, turned his back to the tent, and assumed the attitude of a bored fisherman lost in thought. At least, he hoped that's what he looked like. The traffic noise was too loud to hear what was going on behind him, but after several minutes, he heard a voice coming from his right side.

"Having any luck?" It was Tom and Tim, walking toward the end of the pier, carrying their belongings and a good string of fish.

Charlie wouldn't recognize Tom and Tim if he tripped over them – he had never seen their faces – and he hoped that, with his mode of dress, plus the sunglasses, they wouldn't recognize him either.

"Hadn't had a damn bite all day. Guess you fellas caught 'em all," Charlie responded, gesturing to the catch.

"Jes gotta know how ta set 'em up," Tom rejoined, with a sideways grin.

Charlie shook his head, as the Riley brothers walked on in the direction of the end of the pier. But Tom's words echoed in his head, "know how to set 'em up."

Then it all snapped into place. Plotters. Men in black. Newspaper story listing him as the informant. Set up. They were the ones who had planted the stuff on his boat and tipped the police.

And now they were going to carry out the scheme he had first overheard on the boat.

CHAPTER 17

There was a kaleidoscopic effect caused by the raindrops on the camera lens as it caught the neon lights of South Beach in Miami. From the streaks of blue and green and orange emerged a figure in a royal blue rain parka whose only claim to being a human was a nose and two dark eyes staring out from under the visor. It was clear to the viewing audience that this person had not heard the "on the air" signal from the audio portion being broadcast.

"Goddamn it, they said the storm was coming right through here, and where the hell is it? People ought to hire me as hurricane repellent. Every time they send me out to do the show from storm center, storm center is somewhere else." The voice was that of a wet and windblown James Singer. "This kinda shit doesn't happen to ... Oh, we are?"

"James Singer here on South Beach tracking Hurricane Jorge live. You can see from the level of destruction," he stepped back as the camera panned the area, recording only windblown rain and a few coconut palm fronds blown down on the street, "that Jorge has gone elsewhere. And that's good news for the City of Miami. There's been some airport delay, and traffic was pretty badly snarled when the extra-cautious began to evacuate, but now the all-clear's been given, and this town's getting back to normal. Back to you, Jordan."

Back in the studio, Jordan Faith looked somewhat chagrined, but still dead serious. "That's right, James, Hurricane Jorge has spared the east coast of the U.S. mainland, and for that matter Cuba and the Keys, as it slipped through the Straits of Florida. What we took to be a directional change yesterday turned out to be just a wobble, and the big storm continues on its path along the Tropic of Cancer.

"As we predicted, though, Jorge's power was somewhat diminished as it crossed the Bahamas, and its maximum sustained winds are now clocking at one hundred and fifteen, well within the Category Three range on the Saffir-Simpson Scale. However, now that it's crossed into the Gulf of Mexico, conditions are ideal for strengthening.

"And this may be important," the screen now displayed a graphic of the continental United States. "That front we had hoped would move fast enough to turn the storm north has not only slowed to a crawl, it's also being pushed on a more southerly route by this dip in the jet stream." He pointed to the snake-like ribbon squiggling from somewhere in the Pacific through California and down through New Mexico and Texas and into the gulf before turning north. "If this continues, it could be good news for Texas, but not so good for areas on the northern Gulf Coast.

"In any case, we now put the hurricane at 23.80° north latitude and 81.2° west longitude, and moving about twenty miles an hour. We'll report on the hour, and, of course, interrupt as necessary to keep you up-to-date on this very dangerous storm."

As the screen switched to a graphic of a tropical storm, music suggesting tumult rose to a crescendo.

Jordan Faith looked off in the direction of the chief engineer, and queried, "Do you think maybe we should put the audio from the field on some kind of delay?"

*****

Charlie Cross hadn't been watching the television; he hadn't even thought about it. His little experience on the fishing pier had pushed other thoughts from his mind. Now he sat with Lula on her porch overlooking the gulf, drinking a cold Miller Light. He would have preferred to drink something darker, but as light beer went, Miller seemed to have more taste than most, and he knew that if he kept drinking dark beer, he'd have to buy some bigger shorts.

As he left the pier that afternoon, his head was spinning, and he knew he needed to sort out what was going on and what, if anything, he was going to do about it. What he needed was a confidante; someone he could trust to listen and keep quiet about what was said. Lula came the closest to fitting the description, so he'd stopped off at Tom Thumb on his way home, picked up a twelve-pack, and headed for Lula's. Fortunately, Lula was there and didn't have plans.

The Gulf of Mexico was behaving itself today. That probably meant the wind was out of the north. When that happened, the gulf was a lot more like a pond than the massive body of water it was in truth. Although the beachers didn't like the black flies that seemed to blow in from America, and the surfers sure didn't think much of the absence of breakers, when the conditions were like this, it had a soothing effect if you were just watching. The whole blue-green expanse was flat and calm, and, now and again, it would lap against the sand beach, as if an air bubble had been released somewhere from its depths, risen to the surface, and caused a single ripple.

"Lula, this is gettin' curiouser and curiouser," Charlie began. Because he hadn't ever told her about the night of the four strangers, he led off with that, then reminded her of their misadventure while sailing near the Sandcastle Hotel building site, and tied it all in with the setup with the alleged dope. He ended by recounting today's episode on the fishing pier.

"Whadaya think of that?" he concluded, with the enthusiasm of an encyclopedia salesman wrapping up a deal.

"I just don't know, Charlie," Lula mused, knowing that Charlie wasn't there because he needed directions. "What do you think?"

"I think," continued Charlie, barely pausing for breath, "that those people are crazy, ruthless, and need to be stopped before they do any more damage, or hurt someone." He paused, considering. "But then again, it wouldn't upset me if that big ugly erector-set-looking thing came crashing down right into the sound. In fact," he grinned, "it might make a good artificial fishin' reef."

Lula cut her eyes toward Charlie, pursing her lips. "Zat so?"

"No. I guess it's not. Not really. But what am I gonna do about it?" Charlie didn't wait for an answer before he went on. "I could go to the police and tell 'em that someone was gonna blow up the Sandcastle. And they'd say 'how do you know?' And I'd say 'I heard two guys talkin'.' And they'd say 'who are you?' And I'd say 'Charlie Cross.' And they'd look on their computer and say 'Oh yeah, Charlie Cross the dope fiend. We'll get right on it. And, oh, by the way, were you on acid this time?' Maybe not." He stopped the singsong imaginary repartee with a sober note.

Lula was trying unsuccessfully not to laugh. "Very amusing, Mr. Cross, but they might believe you."

Charlie looked at Lula, raising a skeptical eyebrow. "Right!" He slumped in his chair.

"Perhaps," he ventured after a while, "if the bad guys were made aware that someone knows what they're planning?"

Lula seemed to think about that. "Maybe. If they don't know it's you who knows. They've already proven their willingness to act in defense of their plan. And then what?"

Then what? Charlie thought. "Then what, what?"

"Then, do you suppose they'll just go away?" intoned Lula, Socratically.

"Well, why not?" Charlie rejoined. "They'd know somebody knows their plan. Why would they carry it out and risk being caught?"

"Seems to me that anybody crazy enough to do what they're trying to do might not be scared off so easily. Maybe they'd just try something else – or the same thing – but later. Or maybe they'd try to eliminate the troublemaker." Lula let that hang in the air.

Looks like full circle, Charlie thought as he got up to get them another beer. Sometimes beer helped a person think better.

Watching the red glow off to the west evolve slowly, Charlie sipped yet another beer. They hadn't said much since Lula had suggested the impediments to Charlie's idea.

"Maybe the only way to put a stop to 'em is to catch 'em in the act," Charlie concluded, after much consideration. "But, of course, unless they didn't know you caught 'em, or you had the police right handy, it'd be kinda like playing gotcha with a porcupine."

Lula turned her head toward Charlie. Her

eyes were now shaded in the twilight, but he figured she was looking at him like he was crazy.

"I guess that sounds weird, but to stop 'em cold and permanently, they've got to know that I know and that I can prove it. They've also gotta know that, in the event of my untimely disappearance, the police will be immediately privy to the proof. Does that make sense?"

After a few moments, Lula answered, "Yeah, it does. But I don't see how you're gonna do that."

Later that evening, instead of snuggling Lula off to bed, Charlie finagled a drive down the beach with her in her convertible. It was a weeknight, and most of the bars were either closed or real near to it. The season was passed; even beach people couldn't burn the candle every night.

Charlie wasn't sure what he was looking for, but just thinking about the problem and talking about it with Lula wasn't going to accomplish anything. As they drove away from the last of the cinderblock houses along Via de Luna Drive, the first thing he noticed was an eerie glow coming from the direction they were traveling.

"What is that?" Lula sounded shocked, and there was good reason.

What it was was maybe five or six stories of

superstructure, highlighted by klieg lights. It looked like something out of *The Road Warrior*, an old movie set in a hypothetical post-nuclear-disaster future. Apparently, IQ had decided to throw a little light on the subject of vandalism.

Charlie did not wish to be seen around the Sandcastle site, and promptly did a "180" back to the house. He didn't know what this new development meant, but he had the feeling it was going to be good for his side.

Chapter 18

Jackson Bolton came dangerously close to flipping his executive desk chair over backwards when the telephone rang.

Shortly after his conversation the day before with Slidell Goodbee, a phone company representative had arrived at the Bolton home and office to install additional equipment. The additional equipment looked innocuous enough: a white touch-tone model sitting beside the original telephone on his desk at the office and on the kitchen counter at his home. This particular unit, unlike its mate, had a direct connection with the desk phone of a deputy sheriff assigned especially to monitor any calls coming in over it. Bolton was eying the new phone like a serpent on his desk when the call button on his old phone lit up.

"Mr. Bolton," came the voice of his secretary, "the deputy says you can pick up now."

"Bolton." He tried to sound natural.

"Mr. Bolton, do you know who this is?"

queried the voice on the other end. Jackson Bolton would not ever forget that voice.

"Yes. I believe so. What do you want?"

There was a pause, then, "You know what I want. So listen good. I'm gonna tell you how to give it to me. You'll only get one chance.

"Tuesday night. Twelve midnight. Head east from Pensacola Beach down Via de Luna. The Sugar Bowl. Stop your car. Walk to the center and put the money in the receptacle. Turn around and walk back to your car and leave. One hundred thousand dollars in twenties in a brown shopping bag. Come alone. Don't call the police. Now repeat the directions."

Jackson did as he was told.

"Good," said the voice. "Do this right and I'm outta your life for good. Fuck it up and the building goes boom. And ... who knows what else." The line went dead.

Jackson sat and stared at the receiver. That last little bit sent a shock that numbed his brain. He didn't want to think about what "who knows what else" meant. Maybe he shouldn't have called the sheriff.

The call button on his desk phone lit up again. "Mr. Bolton, the deputy says he got it and you can hang up now. The sheriff will call you back."

Jackson Bolton's mind gradually began to function, but not in any way that might be deemed constructive. In his imagination, he saw the house on Scenic Highway. A figure approached the front door. In the kitchen, Ada was cooking something when the doorbell rang. Don't answer it, he prayed. Call the police. But he knew Ada – she was a smart woman, but too trusting. Despite their conversations about general caution and this recent mess, she would go to the door. A person who would kill Coleman Dunlee for no good reason would surely do her harm if he felt he'd been betrayed. As Jackson saw the door open, he grimaced.

Again, the startle reaction as the call buzzer sounded.

"It's Sheriff Goodbee on line one," explained his secretary.

He shut his eyes hard to clear the waking nightmare and took a deep breath. "Bolton."

"Well, Mr. Bolton, the good news is we recorded the conversation and traced the call. The bad news is the call originated from a pay phone at Pensacola Boulevard and Brent Lane. We had to move cautiously to avoid alerting our extortionist, and by the time our undercover guy got there, no luck."

"So now what?" Jackson said gloomily.

"We'll keep the phone under surveillance and later, maybe tonight, we'll dust it for prints. But I suspect our guy's too smart for that, and God knows how many sets of fingerprints are on that phone. It's near the carwash, and lots of people use it. But who knows?" Slidell sounded wistful.

"As for the drop, this is what I want you to do. Cut up some newspaper and put it in a grocery bag, the kind you have around the house. Use enough paper so it looks like one hundred thousand dollars in twenties, and roll the sack tight at the top. Come Tuesday, do just what the man said. We'll take care of the rest.

"A word of caution. Our bad guy may have a confederate, someone watching you. So you've got to go through the motions just like it was the real thing. Go to the bank and take some money out. Handle it like you might handle a hundred thou in cash. Look over your shoulder. That sort of thing.

"This guy is gonna be real suspicious anyway, and if he gets the idea it's not for real, he won't show. I don't have to remind you, this guy killed your friend just to prove he was serious. We need to nail him on the first go 'round."

"That's right, Sheriff. You don't have to

remind me," Jackson echoed, having a momentary flashback to his previous fantasy.

"If anything out of the ordinary, anything inconsistent with the plan, happens, call me immediately." Slidell gave Jackson his home phone number and direct access number at the office and rang off.

Jackson pulled a quart of expensive tequila from his bottom desk drawer and took a swallow directly from the bottle. There were too many missteps that could bring his waking nightmare to reality.

Maybe there was another way.

*****

Jackson Bolton was not the only one mulling over the pros and cons of this little caper. Miles away, in the bowels of the city of Gulf Breeze, Sonny Banner sat in his own office, elbows planted on his desk, hands joined with the index fingers steepled to the bridge of his nose.

This was too easy, Sonny thought. I am indeed a clever dude. Of course, it could be that Bolton is just a wuss, but that's not the word on the street. No. Bolton has brought the police in, just like I thought, and that's just fine. Sonny smiled to himself. Just like the magicians. Just a little ploy with misdirection.

He had picked the Sugar Bowl for the drop site on purpose. Only a fool would pick the Sugar Bowl. It was an area of pure white Pensacola Beach sand that bowed in the middle and was surrounded by shrub-covered dunes, so that it actually did resemble a giant bowl of sugar. It was bordered by a cul-de-sac and Via de Luna Road. There could be a hundred undercover cops hidden there, and nobody would ever know it. It would be impossible to make good an escape with the ransom money. Slidell Goodbee must have had an erection when he heard the drop site, Sonny chuckled. But that was the plan: let the good sheriff think he was dealing with an idiot. Focus on the Sugar Bowl. Relax a little bit.

While everybody had their eyeballs glued on the drop site, Sonny would be where they weren't looking. Sonny would be riding over to the beach and then back with Jackson Bolton in Bolton's car. He'd give Bolton his own sack, take Bolton's, force him to make the drop, and then let him go when they got back to his own waiting car. Nobody would be watching Bolton after the drop.

The only glitch Sonny could anticipate was that Bolton might see him hidden in the backseat when Bolton got in his car to drive to the beach. But they had two cars: Bolton's new Cadillac Sedan de Ville and his wife's two-year-old minivan. It would be a simple matter to disable the Cadillac, forcing Bolton to drive the minivan to the drop. Hiding in the back of a minivan was a piece of cake.

Yes, Sonny calculated, making money comes easy to a clever dude.

Chapter 19

Flora Edwards stood erect, dressed in a blue jumper with a frilly white blouse – a tall pretty young woman who, at this point in her career, was doing the weather for *Channel 5 News* in Pensacola.

"It'll be sunny and hot in Mobile," she said, pointing to the rather large and easily recognizable divot in the northern Gulf Coast, "and more of the same for the Pensacola area." Again she pointed.

Charlie, stretched full length on Lula's sofa, wondered just what in the hell Flora was pointing at. Nowhere on the Channel 5 map of the Florida Panhandle was there an M-like indentation suggesting Pensacola Bay. This was, after all, a Pensacola station. Why couldn't they get a map that showed Pensacola Bay?

"But don't let these conditions fool you. We've still got Hurricane Jorge out there in the Gulf of Mexico, and it seems to have radically changed course." Flora Edwards flipped to another screen, and had it not been for a symmetrical hole in the middle, it would have looked pure white.

"Since it passed through the Straits of Florida, Hurricane Jorge has taken a turn to the north and slowed majorly. We now have it at 25.9^{o} north latitude and 85.1^{o} west longitude, moving at seven miles an hour in a north-northwesterly direction. This storm now has sustained wind velocity of one hundred and thirty-two miles an hour. Wow! That's a Category Four on the Saffir-Simpson Scale." She smiled again, for no apparent reason.

"If you look here," she changed maps on the screen, "you can see that Jorge's eye is, well, right there, and if I draw a line from there north-northwest, it runs right through here." She drew a line with a magic marker running directly through Pensacola. "At seven miles an hour, we figure Jorge will be in Pensacola Bay sometime Wednesday. Yikes!

"Of course, ya'll know that hurricanes can do funny things. They can speed up, or slow down, or turn right, or turn left, or just do nothing. So we can't say for sure, but maybe you should be thinkin' about what you're goin' to do if Jorge comes a callin'." She smiled again, and the picture switched to an apparently sleeping anchor and a terminally bored sportscaster.

Charlie punched the remote and the screen went blank. Wednesday, he thought. That didn't give him much time. He had to secure the *Long Gone.* Probably Lula would want some help putting up storm shutters. That didn't count dealing with the little group of homegrown terrorists. And where exactly was he going to run when the storm came? He hadn't given it much thought – he supposed somewhere with Lula.

As he looked out at the gulf, he wondered how there could possibly be a monster hurricane just three or four hundred miles offshore. People still frolicked on the sun-drenched pristine sand, and the dark blue water glittered in the distance. The only thing that was different from any other day was the surfers. They littered the breakers like jellyfish in August.

Assuming that Flora was right, which was probably a very dangerous assumption, the terrorists would have plenty of time to do their damage, if Charlie didn't stop them. His plan was simple, or stupid, depending on how it worked out.

Charlie would dig out his old mini-cam, hide near the Sandcastle superstructure, and film the initial preparations for the demolition. He'd then casually walk over to the desperados and advise them that, if they didn't go away, he'd give the film to the sheriff. To avoid the desperate little band deciding that they'd rather just kill Charlie and go on about their terrorism, before he confronted them, he'd hand off the film to Lula for safekeeping. Charlie would be able to accomplish all this in the dead of night because the Sandcastle site was now well-lit, which was what gave him the idea in the first place.

Last night, when he'd explained his scheme to thwart island evil to Lula, she told him he was crazy. Charlie allowed as how they were in agreement on that point, but suggested that somebody had to do something, or there was a good chance that people could get hurt.

Lula, apparently unable to think of a better solution, agreed to participate.

CHAPTER 20

If Santa Rosa Island had been attacked with nerve gas sometime Tuesday morning, it wouldn't have looked much different.

The sun was shining; the wind was moderate; the temperature was warm. But there weren't any people, at least not many. Occasionally, one could be seen ducking back into a house or a condo, like a coyote taken suddenly by the intrusion of civilization.

Driving west on Fort Pickens Road, there was no traffic. Only a single pane of glass was left unboarded for ingress and egress at the western Tom Thumb across from the Sans Souci Condominiums. The marquee at Peg Leg's proclaimed "Everybody Welcome Except Jorge," but that was not the impression a wandering tourist might have. The beach bar was shut tight with plywood siding. The island waited, nervously, for the powerful storm.

The seasoned and the wary were gone to

somewhere on the mainland – with relatives, friends, in motels, or just headed north. A few others were not. Of those who stayed on the island, most were just late leaving due to some last minute island business. These beach denizens were relying on the local weather forecast and luck. After all, Channel 5 said Wednesday, and it was still early Tuesday.

There was also the lunatic fringe, a group of diehards who would not leave the island for any reason. Their prevailing thought was that they had ridden out hurricanes before. They lived. The island's still here. What's all the hubbub?

There were also the "aginers." They were the folks who by nature were just "agin" it, whatever it was. Water fluoridation, a polite request to move so a person might get by in the grocery aisle, orders to evacuate, it didn't matter. They were agin it. These were the people who would jeopardize the lives of the Coast Guard by eleventh hour pleas for rescue.

Then there were the assorted nuts who just didn't seem to grasp the concept that millions of tons of wind-driven water were likely to rush over the island, taking everything but the sand – and sometimes that, too – wherever it chose to take it. These were the people who, when asked why they weren't leaving by the roving TV reporters, would look into the camera and say, "I think it'll be all right. I'm jus' gonna get me some beer and get under the bridge and fish." These were the people who just weren't there after the hurricane. But the island seemed to spawn a new crop of them in time for the next storm.

As the hours passed toward sunset, even the casual observer could sense the difference. The wind velocity increase and the shift from the west to the east were the big clues, but also the approaching clouds – high cirrus at first, then the towering cumulonimbus. The very air for breath became oppressive, as the atmospheric pressure slid down the scale of millibars.

As the last rays of yet another beautiful sunset faded between the horizon and the clouds, Charlie was nailing the final piece of plywood to Lula's second floor sliding glass door. He noted that the beach had suddenly changed personalities. Directly above boiled ominous dark clouds, and the surf had taken on an angry appearance. Never had Charlie seen breakers of this magnitude on the beach. But it was low tide, and they were as yet no threat to the island dwellings.

It was almost as if an undetected northerly adjacent pocket of low pressure was acting as a magnet, gradually building potential to suddenly suck the tempest into Pensacola Bay. Yet, as the island was enveloped in ominous darkness, the local media parroted the National Weather Service observations: Jorge's northward movement was actually slowing. It would most certainly be Wednesday before landfall, and where exactly that would be was still unknown.

Shortly after sunset, eastward down the island, a small army of beach bums – by their appearance – were being deployed in the dunes surrounding the Sugar Bowl. Three surfers sat on the roof of their station wagon, apparently contemplating a midnight ride in the hurricane surf, at the last parking area between the Sugar Bowl and the J. Earle Bowden Way on the road to Navarre Beach. At the eastern Tom Thumb under the water tower that was painted to look like a beachball, a group of workmen appeared to be putting the finishing touches on the hurricane shutters. Nowhere on the east end of Pensacola Beach were sheriff's cruisers in evidence.

*****

The frowning face of James Singer was the first thing the camera found before backing to expose an area of beach that didn't look particularly storm-ravished.

"Folks, we're here on the beach at Panama City, and, as you can see, Hurricane Jorge has yet to make an impact."

The camera panned the area so the TV audience could see what Singer was talking about. It looked like something out of a vacation brochure, only at night. Small breakers rolled in, while gentle breezes ruffled the palm fronds.

"But we're taking no chances. Citizens of Panama City Beach have been through this before, and they know what a hurricane can do. City fathers have issued the order for mandatory evacuation, and set up shelters inland for those who live near the gulf, and, of course, for the homeless. But, as the clock on the wall strikes ten, I'm afraid there's not much to see. Back to you, Jordan."

As the picture faded to black, the viewing audience was treated to what could have been interpreted as James Singer throwing the microphone into the sand.

The scene at the studio was quite different,

almost as if they were expecting another field report. The picture was that of Jordan Faith fumbling with his earpiece, and staring up at nothing with his mouth open. Since Jordan was quite senior, the viewing audience might well have believed they were witnessing a stroke.

Someone in the studio crew must have directed Jordan's attention to the little glowing red light that signified the camera was switched on and that he was on the air, for he animatedly turned toward the camera, as if someone had turned on his switch as well.

"Pardon the dead air, ladies and gentlemen, but I was just getting the latest information about Hurricane Jorge from the National Hurricane Center in Miami. I believe this will be of vital concern, especially to those residents of Pensacola.

"Jorge is now not only well within the Category Four range, with winds in excess of one hundred and forty miles an hour, but it is now beginning to move.

"If you've been watching, you know that Jorge has been meandering north at between five and ten miles an hour. Now we are advised that its speed has jumped to twenty miles an hour and seems to be increasing.

"We can now predict landfall at Pensacola

Beach, but the precise time is still in doubt. If its northerly speed continues to increase, it could be shortly after midnight.

"You can see here is the eye." The TV screen changed to green, with splashes of yellow and red. "These ragged edges are the feeder bands. If the storm continues on its present course, it looks like it will come in just to the west of Pensacola proper. In fact, just about now Pensacola Beach should be experiencing the first of these rain bands."

The picture changed again, and now there was a younger man sitting beside Jordan Faith.

"This is my associate, Dr. Richard Wolfe. Dr. Wolfe has his PhD in meteorology. Welcome aboard, Dick," Jordan said, hitting the last word hard. Faith was unaccustomed to sharing the spotlight with another expert, and, even though he realized he'd have to step down some day, he couldn't shake the feeling he was being rushed. "So tell our viewers what we've got here."

"Well, Jordan, as you know, this is a Category Four hurricane on the Saffir-Simpson Scale," began Dr. Wolfe.

"Why, yes, I do know that, Dick. And, for our audience, that means that it has sustained winds of between one hundred and thirty-one and one hundred and fifty-five miles an hour. Our last clocking on Jorge had its sustained wind at one hundred and forty-five miles an hour. So what does that mean, Dick?"

"Eh ... Richard, please. It means a storm surge of between thirteen and eighteen feet and major damage to coastal areas."

"Yes, that's what the textbooks say, eh ... Dr. Dick," Jordan cut in, "but let's tell the folks something they can use. For instance, Jorge looks like it's going to make landfall at high tide, and that means you can add four or five feet to that tidal surge range. Say between seventeen and twenty-two feet. Considering the water weight per square meter, that'll flatten a beach bungalow. That is, if hundred-and-forty-five-mile-an-hour winds don't blow it away first.

"I'd say if you're not off Santa Rosa Island right now, you sure better get off quick." Jordan Faith looked over his half-glasses at Dr. Richard Wolfe.

Dr. Wolfe just nodded.

*****

As the hour approached eleven, having left Lula's car parked illegally on the shoulder of the road, Charlie and Lula made their way to the scrub-covered knoll near the burial point where island locals sometimes conducted brief ceremonies and spread the ashes of departed loved ones on Santa Rosa Sound.

There was no danger of interrupting a funeral tonight, but the low foliage was a welcome shield against the winds, which now reached forty knots by Charlie's calculation. From this vantage, Charlie could have hit the Sandcastle superstructure with a seashell.

They waited.

*****

Jackson Bolton cussed under his breath. He had just discovered that his new Cadillac had a dead battery. Slamming the door as he exited, he made his way toward Ada's minivan.

Jackson wondered how that would affect the game plan. Would the sheriff be expecting the Cadillac he usually drove? Would some deputy come over to check when a minivan pulled up at the drop site? He could only hope the sheriff would figure it out before the whole plot was blown sky high – there was no time to call the sheriff now. All he could do was go with the flow and hope it was his lucky day.

Jackson was pleased that the minivan cranked right up. This was a good omen. That, plus he had decided to buy a little insurance, so to speak, on his own.

Reasoning that the sheriff's plan would be to arrest the extortionist when he approached the drop site, Jackson believed that the two most likely things to go wrong were that the guy would recognize a trap and not show up, or that he would somehow get the brown bag and disappear.

There wasn't much he could do about the first alternative. He'd have to trust the sheriff. The big downside, however, if the guy somehow got the bag and escaped, was that when he found he had a double handful of newspaper, he'd retaliate against Jackson or his family.

Jackson had decided to safeguard that alternative by actually giving the guy his hundred thousand. If the sheriff caught the extortionist, it wouldn't matter. If he got away, maybe the guy would keep the deal and that would be that.

Something very cold and hard pressed to the back of Jackson's skull, interrupting his thought process.

Unbeknownst to anyone but Dickerson Banner, there had been a slight change in his plan, too.

Sonny had decided it would be great fun to expand his game of "stump the sheriff." He would commit the perfect crime. He would make Jackson Bolton only pretend to put something in the receptacle. Nobody would ever come to make the pick up. But the money would still be gone. How did the crook get away with the money? Law enforcement would long be scratching their heads about that one.

Sonny had also thought it might be better to simply kill Bolton. But then he'd give up his place in crime history.

This way would be much better, and he could always kill Bolton later if there was a problem.

*****

"Don't be a pussy," was Colonel Dubach's response to Tom Riley's protest that the wind was picking up. "We've put a lot of time and effort into this plan, and I'm not going to let a little wind throw us off. Unless, of course, you want out."

"No. No. I'm in. I was just thinking ..." Tom's voice trailed off.

"Now are there any other problems we need to deal with?" Dubach eyed his men.

It had just been the day before when Chou had discovered, inadvertently, that the six floors of steel girders were lighted at night. They had toyed with cutting the electricity, but decided that would attract almost as much attention as blowing the thing up. They had concluded that nobody was going to notice a black-clad figure beside a girder at midnight. Certainly not from the road, and certainly not the sleeping security guard.

Hearing no other objections from the Woolieboogers, Dubach barked, "OK men, let's do it," and off they went to the whaler, now bobbing mightily in the sound.

*****

Fortunately, even the nuts had enough sense to stay off the gulfside beach, but if someone had been there, it would have been awesome indeed. For as it approached the witching hour, the gentle Gulf of Mexico was fast becoming the stormy north Atlantic, its breakers beginning to suggest those of Waimea Beach. The sugar-white sand became millions of tiny propelled missiles, smashing and penetrating even the concrete pylons. The berm, the man-made dune system the Island Authority had hoped would hold back the force of nature, was quickly being torn asunder by the gouging and slashing tendrils of the mighty surf. Above all, the push and roar of the banshee wind.

It was not a good night to be out.

CHAPTER 21

Indeed, it was not a fit night out for man nor beast, nor sheriff's deputies, nor criminals, nor Wooliebooggers, nor citizens just trying to do the right thing. GZZZZSSSH, a noise made by hand-held radios and drive-through order boxes, could just barely be heard over the pandemonium that was Santa Rosa Island, very near the Sugar Bowl.

"Goodbee." Slidell spoke into the hand-held.

"Eh ... Ten-Four, Sheriff. This is Atwood. It's gettin' a little woolly out here. Whadaya think, Sheriff?"

"That's a roger on that, Deputy. Looks like somethin's coming. Let's play it out."

"That's a Ten-Four, Sheriff." Damn, thought Atwood. Sure, duty and all, but this is bullshit, a sentiment shared by all law enforcement on the beach that night.

"Eh, Sheriff, this is Surferboy." That was the code name for the two officers waiting in the parking lot in the direction of Navarre. "Eh,

Sheriff, our dune is going away. Request permission to move."

"That's a negatory, Surferboy. Hold up just a bit. Somethin's comin'." Slidell hated to put his two men in harm's way, but this looked like the showdown. However, if this next guy didn't stop, it was haul-ass time.

*****

After pushing the long barrel of his Smith & Wesson .44 magnum in Jackson Bolton's neck, Sonny had reached up and turned the rearview mirror sideways.

"Mr. Bolton, if you do exactly as I say, you'll walk out of this alive. If you don't ..." Sonny whispered as menacingly as he could, and then pulled the hammer back on the .44 to finish the sentence.

Jackson started to nod, but didn't want to disturb whatever was sticking in his neck. "Whatever you say. I'm no hero."

"Good boy. Now. You drive to the Sugar Bowl, just like I told you. But when we get there, you just pretend you've got something under your jacket and walk to the receptacle. Pretend to put something in it, and walk back and get in the car.

Then we drive back to Pensacola. You let me out with the money, and you go home. Simple, no?"

Again Jackson tried to nod, but instead said, "I understand."

"Yeah, but there's always a catch, right? And here's the catch. If you don't convince me you're carrying a sack of money and putting it down the box, I'm gonna shoot you, and I won't miss.

"Let me explain. What I have here," Sonny jabbed the barrel hard into the base of Jackson's skull, "is a long-barreled forty-four magnum loaded with hollow-point ammunition. If I hit you anywhere, you're a dead man. Understand?"

Jackson answered in the affirmative.

"Now there's another catch. You probably knew there was. And that is, you can't ever tell anybody that you were just pretending or that I was ever in this car. Why, you say? Because that's what I'm tellin' you to do, and if you don't ... Well, use your imagination. You don't know me, but I know you. I know your wife. I know where you live and where you work. I even know what beauty shop your wife goes to." Sonny took a shot in the dark on the last one.

"Do we understand the program here? You do what I say, and you lose one hundred thousand dollars and me, forever. You don't do what I say, and somebody dies. Maybe worse."

No question about it, Jackson understood exactly what to do, and that's exactly what he did.

Once Jackson was back in the minivan, Sonny directed, "Take us home, Lightnin'," and off they went toward Bob Sikes Bridge.

Sheriff Goodbee and company had recognized the minivan as it approached the drop site – now they waited to spring the trap.

*****

Down the beach a little to the east, Charlie Cross was trying to remember what he'd learned in the Navy about stealth. Nothing readily came to him, so, recalling all the war movies he had ever seen, he began a slow belly-crawl toward the superstructure of the Sandcastle Hotel. Lula reluctantly followed suit, cussing Charlie most foully for getting her out here, and alternately beseeching the Almighty to let her live long enough to personally beat the snot out of him.

"Let's get this done and get outta here," screamed Tim. It was no longer necessary to be concerned about being seen or heard. Nobody was on the island, and, if they were, they sure couldn't hear anything.

The Colonel nodded and waved the Wooliebooggers over. Forming them into what looked like a rugby scrum, he yelled as loud as he could.

"Set the charges near the ground. Give us two hours, and let's go. We don't need any lookouts. I'll make sure the boat doesn't blow away, and, Chou, you help out if Tim or Tom needs it."

Tim resented having Chou's help, but this was not the time to argue. They all nodded.

"Let's do it then," screamed the Colonel.

Charlie and Lula had maneuvered their way very near to the activity, Charlie filming all the way. With everything in motion, and no chance of being heard, getting close was no problem. Now the movements of the Wooliebooggers suggested things might be coming to a close.

"OK, Lula. You take the camera, and I'll meet you in the car in just a little bit."

Lula looked hard at Charlie. "You're crazy. We don't have a little bit. We've got to get off this island right now, or they'll close the bridge on us."

Close the bridge on us? Charlie hadn't thought about that. He knew the hurricane wasn't supposed to happen until sometime Wednesday afternoon, but "supposed to" didn't feed the bulldog. Charlie had tried not to think about the squalls that had raked them as they waited by the dunes. But Lula was right. Those were feeder bands, and they were fixin' to meet Jorge face-to-face.

Charlie grabbed the camera with one hand, Lula with the other, and ran. The terrorists would have to wait.

Chou, Tim, and Tom had finished their task and were now moving as a group toward the boat, when they almost ran over the Colonel.

"Hold it, men. We can't use the boat. The water's too rough and the boat's too slow anyway. We've got to get an automobile as quick as possible and get off this island."

For a moment, the three men looked at Dubach as if he'd suddenly gone mentally AWOL. The focus that had been necessary in dealing with the explosives was such that other things, like a hurricane, had been ignored. Almost in unison they suddenly understood, and, like their secret observers, made for the road.

*****

Slidell's deputies were good men, courageous enough to face down armed bad guys every day of the week, but now Slidell was getting calls almost as fast as he could push the receive button. It was time to pull out. Nobody was coming out here in a hurricane, not even for one hundred thousand dollars. He gave the command.

*****

Charlie and Lula had finally fought their way through the wind, which at times threatened to tip them over and roll them into the sound, to Lula's antique Cadillac convertible. At this point, it didn't matter, but Charlie had wished the car wasn't a convertible. Despite its age, the car cranked on the first try, and Charlie tried not to spin the tires in his haste to get out of there. Getting stuck in the sand at that particular moment would not be good.

A rush of relief engulfed Charlie and Lula as they began moving off in the direction of safety, only too soon to be shattered at the sight of four black-clad men standing in the middle of the street hailing them for a ride.

What to do? What to do? There was no question who the men were. They were drug-plantin', buildin'-blowin', probably murderin' terrorists, and the best thing for everybody would be to run 'em down, or, failing that, abandon 'em. But then Charlie looked at Lula and immediately knew neither of them could be quite that coldblooded.

Charlie pulled over. Four wet sweaty Wooliebooger piled into the backseat.

*****

It had only been thirty minutes since Jackson Bolton and Sonny Banner had rolled up to the Bob Sikes Bridge. Rolled up, as opposed to rolled across, because there was a police blockade right in the middle of the street.

As the deputy sheriff approached the minivan, from the rear of the van came a muffled voice. "Don't fuck this up."

The deputy had explained to Jackson that a high-profile vehicle could not make it across the bridge under these conditions. He could park the van and go across last with one of the deputies, or seek shelter on the island. Jackson, to his credit, had told the deputy he'd park the van and probably ride over with the deputies.

For cryin' in a goddamned barrel, Sonny thought. He had other ideas. "I ain't ridin' across no bridge with no deputy sheriff, and I ain't stayin' on this piece o' shit island. We'll wait 'til he leaves and go over. Park this damn thing behind the Visitors Information Center." If he hoped for his plan to work, Sonny couldn't do otherwise.

Finally the deputy left. After giving him time to get across the bridge, Sonny was about to tell Jackson to follow the deputy's route when, off to his right, out of the corner of his eye, Sonny saw one of the most horrible sights he had ever seen – four sheriff's cruisers with their "take down" lights flashing through the storm, headed straight for the minivan.

"Son of a bitch!" Sonny emphasized each word. If he wanted to keep the money and keep out of jail, there was only one thing to do. They'd have to stay on the island, and there was only one place Sonny could think of that might survive a major hurricane – Tristan Towers.

Tristan Towers was a sixteen-story high-rise condominium on the sound side of the island – it had survived several hurricanes unscathed and had been designated a hurricane shelter by the Island Authority. It was sturdy enough to withstand the wind, and a person could get up high enough to avoid the tidal surge. At least, that had been the case with prior hurricanes. However, the other storms had not been full-blown Category Fours. In any case, it was a shelter of last resort – if you couldn't make it off the island.

*****

As Slidell and his small army of deputies approached the bridge, his heart sank. No deputy at the roadblock. That meant it was no longer possible to cross the high bridge between the island and Gulf Breeze without serious risk of life.

It was about this time that Charlie, Lula, and a backseat full of Wooliebooogers arrived. Slidell didn't have much choice, they'd all have to take their chances at Tristan Towers.

Chapter 22

Moving west down Fort Pickens Road toward Tristan Towers, Sonny felt more like he was part of a pinball game than riding in an automobile. The high profile of the minivan was not aerodynamic, and several times it seemed to him that they were in serious danger of flipping. He assumed if in fact that happened, they would surely drown or be sucked out to sea, because the gulf now covered the road.

On his left, Sonny could make out a peculiar tilt to one of the larger condominium structures that sat gulfside. He knew that what this usually meant was that the tide was undercutting the sand from the structure, and, if it continued, sooner or later the building would just crack and fall over into the surf. Amazingly, some of the smaller individual units appeared to be holding their own. Of course, it was dark, and Sonny couldn't tell for sure.

Sonny's awareness of the mayhem coming

down all around him was in the nature of a forced distraction. His major concern really was how the original game had changed. Get in; get the money; get out. Nothin' to it. Now things were different.

Sonny figured it was highly improbable that he could wait out the hurricane with Jackson Bolton without Jackson being able to identify him later. It looked like he was going to have to kill him after all. However, Sonny realized that if Tristan Towers was the only shelter on the island, probably the sheriff and his posse would be coming along shortly. Although Jackson would definitely have to go, he'd wait up on that. He might need a bargaining chip.

As they slowly approached the high-rise, Sonny noticed that the electronic gates had been closed. This was bad. He didn't want to leave the minivan on the street, what there was left of it, because he didn't want the sheriff to see it and he didn't want it washed out into the sound by the tidal surge. He'd need it for a getaway.

When Jackson looked doubtful as they approached the gate, Sonny ordered him to drive through it. That hadn't proved too difficult. Sonny directed him to park somewhere behind the edifice.

Apparently in some sort of effort to conserve plywood, the rear of the building facing the sound had been left unboarded. The idea, Sonny figured, was that the lee of the building would protect the windows. Whatever. It was good news for them. They entered the building.

Sonny had assumed it would be pitch black, but he was wrong. The emergency lighting bathed the whole interior in an eerie red, like a brothel. However, the emergency power source didn't seem to extend to the elevators, so they made their way to the fire stairs. Neither man was in particularly good shape, and after several switchbacks of stairs, Sonny decided the fifth floor was high enough. A good hard kick, and Sonny and Jackson had their own condo to wait out the storm.

During the ordeal, Jackson had docilely followed instructions; he didn't have much choice. He had been hoping for some divine intervention, but now he realized that this just wasn't his day. This man was a ruthless killer, and he had seen his face. Things were looking grim for Lightnin' Bolton.

*****

In fairly short order, Slidell Goodbee, seven deputies, four Wooliebooggers, and Charlie and Lula followed the route of Sonny Banner and Jackson

Bolton. They had detoured, however, on the third floor, deciding that was high enough.

The sheriff had not failed to notice the battered entry gate, but assumed it might have been storm damage. The presence of the minivan hadn't registered. As far as Slidell knew, Jackson Bolton had headed for the mainland long ago; he wasn't looking for his car on the island.

No sooner had the odd little group of wet and frightened wayfarers started to adjust to the howling storm than the telephone rang. For a moment, they exchanged curious looks.

"Goodbee," the sheriff answered, wondering just who might be calling and how they had gotten through. Hurricanes were funny things.

"Sheriff," the voice of one of his deputies came on, "we tried to raise you on the two-way, but I guess the storm interfered." There was a pause.

"Just how did you know where to call, Deputy?" Slidell was mystified.

"Well, Sheriff, it seems Tristan Towers has an infrared sensor system that activates surveillance cameras when someone breaches the perimeter. The security people called us, and that's how we knew where to call you. That's the good news.

"The bad news is you're not alone in the building. There are two men in unit five-ten. One of 'em has a gun, and the other one's Jackson Bolton."

Now there was a longer pause as Slidell absorbed this new development and formulated a plan.

"We'll take care of this end. There's nothing much you can do 'til Jorge blows itself out. But be ready with backup and a Medevac helicopter, just in case things don't go well. There's a good chance communication will go. So get here as soon as the weather allows." Slidell replaced the receiver and turned to his deputies.

Slidell summed up the situation to those present, then gave his instructions. "This'll go down just like a drug bust. There's one way in and one way out. Atwood, you kick in the door. Then we go in fast. They don't know we're here, so we'll have surprise on our side. Any questions?"

There were none. They knew the drill.

"You guys should all know what Jackson Bolton looks like, but if you don't, he'll be the one without the gun. OK. Let's go." Slidell moved toward the door.

As they crept up the staircase, Slidell thought about his deputies. They were tired, wet, and in the middle of a major hurricane. A person would think somebody might have bitched, but no one had. Kinda made him proud.

With the exit of Slidell and the seven deputies, Charlie, Lula, and the Wooliebooggers were left alone. Of course, since the sheriff had no idea what the Wooliebooggers had done, there was no reason not to leave them. However, since Charlie and Lula did know what they had done, it made conversation for them awkward. And since the Wooliebooggers didn't know that Charlie and Lula knew what they had done, they couldn't exactly conduct a *post mortem* on their mission. So they all sat and eyed each other suspiciously as the hurricane's fury increased.

*****

Two floors up, the scene was similar. Sonny didn't want to make friends with a guy he was going to kill, and Jackson didn't want to ask what Sonny intended for him; he might tell him.

In the hall outside the fifth floor unit, Slidell and his men moved cautiously toward the designated door. They prepared for entry by using hand signals, but that really wasn't necessary as a security measure. Sonny couldn't have heard a scream over the howling roar of the wind. The fact of the matter was that the deputies couldn't hear if they were making noise either, as they scuffled toward unit 510.

*****

The TV camera zeroed in on Dr. Richard Wolfe. Apparently Jordan Faith was taking a break. Older guys were like that.

"And there he is," the screen had now switched to a radar image superimposed over an outline of Escambia and Santa Rosa Counties. Dr. Wolfe was pointing at the dark circle in the middle of the green. "That's the eyewall, right now moving over Pensacola Beach.

"Of course, we don't know about the tidal surge, but the National Hurricane Center indicates the wind velocity has declined. Now Hurricane Jorge has been reclassified as a Category Three on the Saffir-Simpson Scale. Sometimes, for reasons only hurricanes know, that happens." He chuckled. "Just before they make landfall, they diminish in power. Maybe because the ocean floor rises. Who knows? But that's good for the City of Pensacola."

*****

Sonny sat trying to figure a way out of this mess.

He knew the sheriff was probably somewhere in the building. Maybe after the storm ended, he'd leave. Sonny could make a break for it then, but there'd be police all over the island checking the storm damage. They were sure to stop him, and if they didn't arrest him then, they'd definitely have his description. They'd find him eventually if he stayed in Pensacola. Damn. He hated that. He liked Pensacola. But there you go – fate works in funny ways.

In any case, he'd have to take out Bolton before he left Tristan Towers. Maybe he could make it look like an accident, but ...

Just then the wind stopped, and a quiet that made his ears ring descended the whole island. What Sonny could hear was the sound of shuffling footsteps outside his door. Sonny hadn't been a criminal all his life for nothing. Bad shit was fixin' to come down if he didn't do something real fast.

Like the strike of a rattlesnake, Sonny grabbed Jackson Bolton by the shirt collar and jammed the .44 in his throat.

"Sheriff, I know you're out there. Kick the door and Bolton dies," he screamed, then fired a shot into the ceiling. "That was a warning. The next one's in Bolton's head."

The silence returned.

Well, so much for that plan, mused Slidell. Now what?

That was pretty much what Sonny was thinking, too. The noise. Where did the noise go? Then the obvious dawned. They were in the eye of the hurricane, and now was his chance to run. If he could make it across the bridge to Gulf Breeze before the back of the eyewall got there, he might have a chance to put some distance between him and the law while the sheriff was waiting out the rest of the storm. Now was the time for action and, if anything, that was Sonny's forte.

"We're comin' out, Sheriff. Move your men back." Sonny was still screaming. There was another silence, then, "I mean it, Sheriff. I'll kill this sumbitch before you can blink."

Slidell didn't really doubt him. "OK. We're backin' off. Don't hurt him."

At Sonny's order, Jackson Bolton opened the door slowly. Slidell and his deputies stood just in front of the fire exit. Sonny eased out the door, the big gun barrel – trigger cocked – under Bolton's chin.

"Here's the deal." Sonny spoke loudly but with frightening calm. "Me and Bolton go out the door. I let him go at the bridge. Anybody tries to stop us, Bolton dies." He paused to let the message sink in. "Sheriff, you know I don't have nothin' to lose." Sonny smiled to himself. "Can only execute a man once."

Slidell understood all too clearly. Bolton was a dead man. The question was, would it be now or later? But since dead was dead, Slidell calculated, he'd play for time. Who knows?

He ordered his men back, and Sonny moved into the stairwell.

CHAPTER 23

Down two flights from the action, the little party of locals continued their silent vigil – of each other. Suddenly the roaring cacophony outside ceased, like somebody turned on the lights in a dark room. However, the building's emergency power didn't do anything for the individual units, so it was still a dark room, and that made the silence all the more intense.

Chou was about to say something about the hurricane eye, when the report of the .44 magnum came echoing through the vent system.

"What was thet?" Chou said instead.

"Given the situation, I'd guess it was a gunshot," answered the Colonel matter-of-factly.

Then silence.

Charlie couldn't stand it. "I'm going to see."

"Charlie, I don't think you ought to," cautioned Lula.

Charlie shrugged off the warning. "I'll be careful. I just don't want to sit here waitin' for some crazy person to come runnin' in killin' people."

The Wooliebоogers didn't say anything. They didn't seem to be much interested in locating the source of a gun that might make such a loud noise.

Once out of the dark unit, Charlie noticed that the common area still glowed red from the emergency system. He moved toward the fire exit door. His dilemma was whether to open the door quickly and dodge back in at the first sign of immediate trouble, or open it slowly and take a chance that someone wasn't standing out there watching it inch open. He opted for the former.

*****

When Sonny and Jackson passed the first switchback down the stairs and could no longer see the fifth floor door, Sonny shoved Jackson to the forefront.

"Move your ass or I'll blow it off."

Jackson took the hint, and the pair moved pall-mall down the staircase.

Just as Jackson passed the door on the third floor landing, with Sonny close behind, Charlie lurched through the opening, slamming Sonny hard backwards into the wall.

Knowing in his heart that he had just slammed the High Sheriff of Escambia County with a fire door, Charlie reluctantly surveyed the damage. But what he saw was Sonny Banner holding a very large gun in one hand and a bloody nose in the other while blinking dumbly at Charlie.

"The gun. The gun. Get the gun," shouted Jackson excitedly.

From his old Navy training and many detective movies, Charlie knew that the best way to deal with a revolver was to insert a finger, preferably a thumb, between the hammer and the firing pin. He lunged.

Whap! Sonny brought the long barrel down on Charlie's head, and Charlie knew no more for a bit.

Jackson, seeing his only hope splayed on the concrete floor, bolted for the fire exit on the second floor – like lightnin'. Fortunately, it wasn't locked, and he never looked back.

Sonny almost fired off a shot in frustration, but quickly reevaluated the situation and made his way rapidly toward the ground floor exit and the minivan.

*****

As Slidell watched the fire exit door close behind Sonny and his hostage, he paused to reflect. It was then that he recalled the minivan parked near the back exit.

He knew he couldn't chase after Sonny without jeopardizing Jackson. The only hope he had was to get a shot at the fleeing felon in the parking lot as he made for the minivan, assuming he had released Jackson.

Sprinting back to the unit where Sonny had been, Slidell grabbed a barstool and quickly smashed the glass from the window. Slidell was an excellent marksman, but five floors up? At night? What choice did he have?

Sighting his .9mm along the shattered windowsill, he watched in astonishment as a lone Sonny Banner ran from the building toward the van. Where was Jackson Bolton? But at least he'd have a clear shot.

Sonny stopped to open the minivan's door, as Slidell knew he would have to. Slidell squeezed off a round.

Blam! Zing! The bullet hit the pavement and whined off in the direction of Gulf Breeze.

Of all the times to choke, Slidell recriminated, coming close to slapping his forehead with the lightly smoking gun. What the hell – he emptied the clip in Sonny's direction as Sonny cranked the van and sped out of the parking lot, spewing brine in all directions.

"Made it," Sonny exalted, as he tried his best to accelerate in the direction of the Bob Sikes Bridge. The gulf had now completely flooded the road.

*****

"Ya know, Richard," Jordan Faith began. The camera was focused on him as he and Dr. Wolfe sat viewing another TV screen on the desk between them. Jordan was plumb tuckered and he looked it. He was ready to let bygones be bygones. "I think that storm is actually gaining speed and power. It's not supposed to do that over land."

Dr. Richard Wolfe just shrugged.

*****

Charlie Cross sat up abruptly as the trailing eyewall slammed into Pensacola Beach. He didn't realize yet that it wasn't only the sound of the hurricane's fury that was causing his head to hurt.

He made his way back to the third floor, where the entire group was now reassembled, huddled by candlelight in the unit where they had initially sought refuge.

*****

Dickerson Banner was beginning to accelerate as he entered the initial upslope of the Bob Sikes Bridge.

He couldn't know in the dark that the trailing eyewall of Hurricane Jorge was accelerating also, but faster. At just about the time Sonny reached the top of the hundred-foot apex of the bridge and saw the lights of the Santa Rosa Yacht and Boat Club, the full force of the hurricane was rudely visited upon him.

*****

Prentiss Mendenhall opened one eye to note the slithering arrival of the leaden light of Wednesday morning.

When Mrs. Mendenhall and her little farm brood had last shut their eyes, it had been under the threat of Hurricane Jorge, landed and headed directly toward her little town of Atmore, Alabama. Of course, they were a good hour out of Pensacola, and the hurricane had lost strength, yet it was still a powerful storm spawning tornadoes as it traveled north.

She was relieved, then startled, by the flurry of footsteps from the hallway. It was her youngest son.

"Momma. Momma. You'll never guess what that ol' hurricane's doin'."

She started to explain that the hurricane was over, but decided it was too much effort. "What, honey? Tell me."

"Momma, it's rainin' twenty dollar bills all over our farm."

EPILOGUE

And what of the sleepy little community of Pensacola Beach?

Well, after the hurricane, it was semi-miraculously still there. But then, why wouldn't it be? Santa Rosa Island had been around since recorded history, and there was no reason to suspect it was going to be run out of Florida by a hurricane anytime soon.

Of course, Jorge, like his predecessors, made some modifications. The people who know these things say there were two fifteen-foot tidal surges that raked the island. That moved some things around; mostly sand though, which will eventually get back to wherever it's going.

The only building on the island seriously damaged was the superstructure of the new Sandcastle Hotel. The Island Authority was quoted as saying "it must have just been blown away."

Charlie Cross and Lula Vidalia weathered the storm. Charlie's boat, the *Long Gone*, wasn't – long gone, that is. Lula had lots of sand deposited under her house. Charlie Cross would have you believe it was most of the beach, but he got it all out – under Lula's strict supervision.

The sheriff and his lady survived nicely. Daphne had taken the kids to her parents' home in Tallahassee, and only experienced remnants of the big storm.

The sheriff continues to keep an eye out for a criminal named Dickerson Banner, but these criminal derelicts blow in and out with the beach breezes.

The Wooliebooger Militia went inactive.

After Charlie Cross explained to them that he had a film he was going to give to Slidell Goodbee if he heard of any more odd occurrences around the Sandcastle property, they elected to become nonviolent. They did decide, though, that Charlie was a pretty good guy after all, what with rescuing them and not ratting them out. So they made Charlie an honorary Wooliebooger and their poker fifth.

William Norton still makes big bucks representing alleged criminals. He also now holds a mysterious videotape with sealed instructions, only to be opened in the event of the death of Charlie Cross. He believes the video is somehow related to the cocaine case, but doesn't really care. Since he is not getting paid to hold the tape, his major interest is helping Daphne Fairhope pass the bar exam so he can entrust the tape to her.

Jackson Bolton was discovered after the hurricane subsided. He was pretty wet, but no worse for wear. Seems the unit where Jackson had taken refuge lost a window, causing the floor to be rapidly inundated. Jackson had hidden under the bed.

Jackson did build his high-rise hotel and condominium resort compound, and it really doesn't look bad at all. It's a lot nicer than the other developments that came in immediately after the Sandcastle was completed.